EYE OF AN EAGLE

A PETER POPPIN ADVENTURE

— JANET HAFNER —

Lulu Publishing Services rev. date: 11/8/2016

DEDICATED to my sons and grandchildren who inspire my writing and to my husband who encourages my every adventure.

CHAPTER ONE

"I don't know, Patches, this cliff falls off right away. Steep, slippery and rocky. What do you think?"

"Ruff, ruff, rrrruff." His tail swings wildly beating the air. His paws tap out an excited dance.

"Quit it, dog. I know you're ready to go."

I've got to get down to the beach while it's still daylight. If I don't, I won't find the driftwood I need to carve that mermaid for Ma's birthday. I hope this beach will give me the wood I need. North and south of here, the Maine coast is nothing but sheer cliffs – no beaches, no wood.

Pa told me yesterday that I need to take chances now that I've turned thirteen. He always encourages me. Ma, on the other hand, is afraid I'm going to get hurt. Everything she says begins with 'don't' or 'be careful.' She'd hate what I'm about to do.

Those giant black patches make the sky look wicked, and the jagged clouds are ready to dump rain. The wind is strong enough to launch a hurricane. It's pushing me all over the place. Can't even keep the hair out of my eyes. Sounds like a hundred hissing snakes. If it gets any stronger, it could blow me off the cliff. For now, all I know is I've got to get down to that beach. Besides, if I find what I need, I can look for some of the buried treasure that town-folk always talk about. They say pirate ships sank off this very shore. Wouldn't it be great if I found something? Yeah . . . but first, the wood.

Can't put it off any longer. It's now or never.

"Ready, Patches? One long deep breath is all I need.

"One . . . two . . . three. Let's go, dog."

With my first step, Patches is off. Then I run straight into a bearberry bush.

"Ouch!" I jerk my leg away. Too late. It got me. Pale green thorns dot my knee. I pull the thorns out as best I can. Tiny red dots take their place. A stinging sensation creeps around my knee and down my calf and shin. Blood's running down my leg. The spots are mighty itchy. What a mess – now my stocking is blood-red. When I get home, Ma's thick, sticky, stinky goo will stop the itch. I hate the smell, but it works. The goo will take care of the itch, but Ma's going to be fighting mad about my stocking. Geez, I can't stop scratching. I have to forget it for now and focus on finding that wood. Got to keep going and make sure I don't run into any more bushes like that.

I'll need more daylight. The longer path would have been safer, but slower . . . nah, this is good. More dangerous, but faster. This wet gravel won't stay put. Pieces fly everywhere. Ouch, ouch.

These granite rocks are as slippery as oil. Hard to balance. Can't steady myself. I'm wobbling and sliding. Maybe I should sit. There's nothing to grab onto. If I could just jab my foot between these rocks, I'd . . . Wow! That was close.

I'm just about at the bottom. Can't see Patches anywhere. "Here boy. Where are you?" He's better than I am on this slope. I bet he's down on the beach already.

Must be the way the old settler, Mr. Whiskers, felt when he tumbled down the cliff. They said he broke every bone in his body. I don't know for sure if it was every bone, but I'm sure it was a lot. At least he didn't die.

Wow - dirt, rock, gravel, twigs, prickly plants - like a blanket spread out from here to the bottom. Got to tackle this on my feet. "I'll just go for it."

That's it. Oh, oh! Picking up speed. Easy. Too fast. Slow down.

"Oooooow."

Thump. That hurt.

I made it. What a slope! Sand's a lot softer on the butt. Better than those jagged rocks. Bet my butt's black and blue.

"Ruff, ruff, ruff."

"Hey boy, there you are. You got down that slope a lot faster than I did. Good boy."

Those nasty holes and scratches on my knee stopped bleeding. I should've worn long pants.

Whose idea was it anyway to go the steep way? Dumb, if you ask me. I could have died.

The ocean looks angry – dark blue-green with whitecaps. I'm glad I have this wide stretch of beach. The last two storms dumped wagon loads of wood on it. Lots of carvers come here looking for sun-bleached driftwood. The mermaid I want to carve for Ma has a long tail – the wood needs to be perfect for that tail. Oak, maple of fruitwood just won't do.

Pa would know where to search, but since he's not here, I'll figure it out on my own. I really wanted my friend, Marian, to come with me. She wasn't in school yesterday or today, so I'll just figure it out on my own.

"Ruff, ruff."

"I'm sorry, boy. I didn't know you were listening. I'm not alone, am I? I have you. When your tail wags like that I know you like what I said. You like me to scratch behind your ears, don't you. I know that look. Those giant black eyes are telling me you're ready - now all I have to do is decide what's next."

I'm not sure my friend, Marian, could have made it down this slope. Maybe it's better that she's not here. Better that Patches is my partner.

When that wind whips across the sand, I swear it's telling me to dig. Why not? A few minutes can't hurt. Maybe I'll find something – rubies, emeralds, gold coins – hundreds of them, enough to fill a wagon. The men in the village talk a lot about pirate ships that attacked schooners sailing from England to Maine. Boy, would I like to find something like a key to a buried chest or better yet, I'd like to meet a pirate. I'd convince him to take me with him on his ship as a cabin boy or deckhand. Don't think Ma would take much to that idea.

Ugh! Gnats – thousands of them. Hate when they fly up my nose. Feels like they're being sucked into my lungs. What's that stink? Smells like a rotten animal. The beach is full of nasty seaweed – smelly stuff.

"You don't like that smell either, boy, do you? Between the gnats and that smell, we'd better find a different place to dig.

"How about here?" Patches cocks his head to the right and shakes his rump. "Okay, boy, I'll dig right here."

My fingers will tell me when I've found something. The wet coarse sand slips through my fingers. Nothing but rocks and seashells. I'll try again.

"Hey, wait a minute, I've got something, Patches."

Dang, my shirt's caught on a branch. Maybe if I twist and move my arm . . . I'm not going to let go of this. These branches don't want me to have it. It must be something valuable.

Got it. Darn. Nothing but a shell covered with barnacles.

This spot closer to the pile of wood looks good. I'll dig a little more. Patches is already digging. Is he going to find something before I do? I dig faster. My fingers strike something solid.

"Come here boy. I think this time I've really found something." Doesn't feel like it's a seashell. Almost feels like cloth. I dug once before on this beach with Pa but never found anything. I hope this time it's a treasure. Got to gently pull it out of the sand. Don't want to destroy whatever it is. Got it.

This is crazy. Looks like a piece of blue cloth wrapped around some kind of object. Let's see if I can peel this back. Good. It's some kind of box. It has a top and bottom, but it won't open. It's not covered with barnacles, and it's not rusty, so it couldn't have been in the water too long. I wonder where it came from. How did it get here? Who buried it? Who does it belong to? I can't believe I found something. I really found something. Wait till I get it home. I'll bet anything it was buried by pirates. Can't go home now to show it to anyone – have to wait. Boy, will they be surprised. Can't wait to yell, "I found buried treasure." I like the sound of those words.

Light's almost gone. At this time of year, it gets dark early. I've wasted too much time. It's the wood I'm after. Can't be too big. Needs to fit under my jacket so I can sneak it into the shed.

Got to remember, this whole trip is about making Ma a mermaid for her birthday. As for this box – I'll just stuff it in my pocket for later. Perfect. It really is weird though. When I hold it, my fingers go numb. Strange. Wood, the wood. Think about the wood. Daylight's disappearing.

The wood is always drier up closer to the cliff. The tide might not get up that far. Dry wood is always better for carving. If the piece I need is wet, I'll have to let it dry before I can work on it and I wouldn't have it ready in time for Ma's birthday. Got barely a month.

The hardest part of the mermaid I sketched is the long flowing tail. The piece has to be about a foot long and not quite as wide – maybe eight inches.

Doesn't look like anyone's been to this beach in a while. Lots of piles to the north, not so much south of here. Nothing but sand, gnats, seaweed, piles of wood, and . . . me.

I'll start here then move north.

"Hey, what the . . . I didn't see these footprints before. From the size of them, a couple of men must have been here. Whoever they are, they've got big feet, but . . . I haven't seen anyone. I guess they were here at low tide. They look like fresh tracks."

Patches sniffs at the footprints then lets out a deep bark.

"Ruff, Ruff. Rrrrrrrrrrrrfff."

"What do you smell, boy? These tracks seem pretty fresh. Do you know who made them?"

Pa taught me a lot about animal tracks when we went hunting. These are people tracks but I still know what to look for. Could those guys be up on the bluff?

"I don't believe it. Two guys are up there. One's tall, the other - short. The short one is heavy. Bet these deep footprints belong to him." Patches sees them. His bark is different. More of a warning – for me and for them.

I didn't know anyone was up there. Looks like the tall one's wearing a long evening coat. How strange. Maybe they would hear me if I shouted. Nah – this howling wind and the rolling surf are too loud. I wonder if they've been up there watching me all this time. Got to tell Pa about them. That's our land up there. They shouldn't be there.

Forget the men. Forget the box. Forget everything – get to the wood. I'm here for that – nothing else. And it's got to be special. There's nothing on this side. Maybe if I go around to the other side, I'll be able to see what's behind that huge log. Is that the piece I need? I think it might be. Darn, it's on the very top. It's beautiful - almost pure white like the sheets Ma hangs on the line. How am I going to reach it? It's way over my head. I'll climb. I'm good at that. I've had lots of practice in the woods.

It's really hard to get a footing with all this kelp and seaweed. The piece I want is behind that log. First, I'll put my foot on this dark piece, then I'll be able to get to that sturdy-looking branch. I can almost touch it. That huge log is in my way. I'll have to push it to the side before I can nudge the one I need out of its hiding place. Ugh! Impossible. Maybe with one good shove, it'll be mine.

I need a couple more steps. Oh, oh, this one doesn't feel strong enough to hold me. Darn, everything's moving. Can't stop it. Gonna fall.

"No, no, no! Yeeeeeouch, oooooooow – oooooow – ooooh – my eye! My eye. Oh God, my eye. Aaaaaah! Pa . . ."

Something really sharp got me. Feels like it went through my eye into my brain – maybe it came out the back of my head.

"Ahoooooooo, ahoooooooo." Patches' howl sends a chill through me.

"Where are you, boy? Help me, Patches, help me."

"Ruff, ruff, ruff, ruff. Ahooooooooooooo."

"Ooooooow – darn, can't open my eye." It's on fire. Can't even feel if my eyeball is there. My arms are pinned down and it feels like rope is holding my legs to the sand. It's all that wood that's on top of me.

"Ruff, ruff, rrrruff. Haah, haah, haah."

"I'm here, boy." Hard to catch my breath.

"Ruff, rrrruff."

"Where are you, boy. Help me."

Can't get my hands loose. Everything's on top of me - wet driftwood, seaweed, logs and kelp. It's too heavy to move. Can't breathe – have no air. I'm stuck, really stuck. Too much to move. Can't budge anything. Can't stop my legs from shaking. I'm scared. I'm more than scared, but

I don't remember the word – *terri* . . . terrified, that's it. God, what did I do. How am I going to get free?

"Oh, God. Help me. Someone. Anyone. Get me out. Help – get me out of here. Help."

Patches scratches and paws at my wooden prison. He wants to get to me.

"Hah-hah-hah-hah." Poor dog, he's panting so hard trying to get to me. I'm under all this wood. I can't see him and he can't see me. Maybe he's going to make more wood fall on me. Better tell him to stop.

"No, Patches, no. No, boy, no." The pawing stops.

"Nnnnnnnn, nnnnnnnnnn, nnnnnnnnnnn," he answers. I hate when he whimpers. He does that when he's not sure what to do.

I should have told someone where I was going. Too late now. No one knows I left. No one knows where I went! How about those men on the cliff? Maybe they're still there. Can't see up there, but I can scream, "Hey, help me. Help. Help. I'm alone. I'm stuck."

If I try to look with one eye, everything is spinning. Got to tell myself not to feel the pain. That's impossible. I hurt all over.

Nobody's here and nobody's coming. I'm in trouble. Real trouble. I can't see the water, but my ears will tell me how close it is. Sounds like the tide is coming in. Now what?

I don't know how Ma and Pa stayed calm when their schooner was caught in a squall between England and here. I was very young. When Pa tells the story he says I was about three. Funny, I don't remember it. Pa told me how giant waves tossed the ship around like a paper boat. The sea took some of the crates that were on deck. Ma says she was sick – just about all the women and children threw up. But . . . they got through it. They survived.

I have to be strong like they were. Can't panic. I'll get through this.

The tide splashes cold salty water in my face. A lot of sand makes the water sting when it beats against my cheeks. My body is shaking and my teeth sound like rocks banging against each other. The cold wind makes me shake. Maybe if I shake hard enough, some of this wood will fall off.

If I don't get myself out from under all this wood, I'm a goner. No . . . no . . . absolutely not. I can't give up. I won't.

I know one thing for sure. I don't want to drown. If I drown, I won't be around to do anything. Won't help Pa in the store or Ma around the house. Won't do anything. Won't ever see Marian again. I'll just be dead.

This can't be real. Is it a dream? One thing for sure – I can't move anything. That's real. I've got to stay alive long enough for Pa to find me.

Think of what Ma and Pa and all our neighbors went through to get to this new land. They didn't give up and neither will I.

Water covers my face, runs down my neck and seeps in behind my shirt. I'm under all this wood, but my clothes are soaked. I'm freezing. This cold is exhausting me.

What can I try? How can I do this? I must figure this out. If I don't, I'll be a gonner.

Pa would say, "Think, Peter."

I'll try to move my knees up, then push. Not enough. I think something moved a little. Try again. My muscles have to work overtime. Can't. My legs are exhausted.

What will happen first? Drown or Freeze. Probably freeze.

That's stupid. Got to stop thinking about dying. Pa would tell me to think positive.

Now my nose is running. Snot and tears – a mess. Can't wipe my face. If I pull this way, maybe I'll free my hands. Not possible.

If the surf comes in far enough, it could lift all this wood and take me along with it - right out to sea. Then I could swim back. It'd be better than this. What's going to happen at high tide?

I refuse. I refuse to drown. Got to keep trying. Can't quit. But . . . what if this is it?

Tiny snatches of air reach my lungs. For a moment I let go and imagine Pa's spirit. What's next, Pa?

Above the roar of the waves, I hear Patches. I listen to his whimpering. "Nnnn – nnnn – nnnn." He knows I'm hurt.

"It's going to be okay, Patches. I almost forgot about you. You have to help me, boy. You have to go and get Pa. Go home, Patches, go home. Get Pa."

"Ruff, Ruff, Ruff." I hope that means he understands.

"Go, Patches, get Paaaaa . . ., bring . . . him . . . here." My voice is weak against the rumble of the waves.

I remember Pa telling me to take my time. He said I shouldn't jump at the first idea. I have to think it through. He always says, "Control the nerves, next, push with spirit and maybe, just maybe, you'll win the battle."

"I will, Pa, I will," I mumble into the wind.

CHAPTER TWO

The water's deeper now. My wet woolen pants are heavy. My jacket too. Everything's waterlogged. Clothes weigh a lot when they're wet and my head feels like it's buried under a bag of sand. Takes all the strength I have to move it. With these clothes, I'd never be able to swim. I'd sink to the bottom of the ocean. Nope, I won't let that happen. Pa's going to come for me, I know it.

All these tears make it hard to see with my left eye and that's the good eye. Can't wipe it. My eye is crusted with salt water and its burning. My hands are finished – they're no longer part of my body. Can't feel them. My face feels strange – caked with blood and sand and ocean junk. I can taste my tears. Got to stop crying. It's not helping.

Brrrrrr. I'm so cold. Guess I can't do anything but shiver. I guess I'm like Patches when he shakes off water.

Got to fight. Can't give up.

"No . . . no . . . no" Got to keep saying that word.

No moon. Fog is rolling in. If it gets like pea soup, no one will find me.

Shouts. Distant. Now I can hear them. Voices. Don't know exactly whose. Might be Pa.

"I'm here, Pa. I'm here – down here . . . at the bottom of the cliff, on the beach."

"Ruff, ruff. Ruff, ruff."

That's Patches. He did it. He got Pa. If I stretch my neck, maybe I can see him through the slits between all this driftwood. I think I hear Pa's voice and a lot of . . . Got to twist a little more. I can make out part of the slope through the cracks. Lights - torches. Rocks falling. They're sliding, just like I did. Yep, I hear him. That's my Pa. He's roaring my name. His voice is so loud, I can hear him over the sound of the surf.

"Peter, Peter, I'm here." That's Pa all right. I'd know his voice anywhere. A giant tremble begins at the top of my head and travels to my little toe. Got to catch my breath and yell as loud as I can.

My voice doesn't sound like me. My voice sounds strange. It stretches out – real slow like a sheep baaaing.. "Oh, get me ooooooo . . . out of here, Paaaa . . . help me."

"I'm here, Peter, I'm here. You're going to be all right, son." Pa's voice is hoarse. Wish I could open both eyes, but I can't. I turn my head a little. I see a figure on the otherside of the wood. I'm choking. Got to get air.

Water splashing. They're trying to get to me. Water deeper. I suck air and my chest burns like a forest fire. My mouth is filled with salt-watery grit. I hear the waves. Sounds like they're coming faster – rolling onto each other.

"Hurry, Pa. Hurry." The water hisses. The waves tug at the pile of wood on top of me. It's trying to suck me out. I feel it pulling on my body. It wants to take me with it.

"No, no, I won't go with you," I scream.

"Peter, Peter, be calm. We're going to get you out of this mess. You're going to be all right." His giant hand squeezes my shoulder. I know that squeeze. It's my father's strong hand. I don't have to open my eyes. I listen to my father's comforting words. "Peter, you're safe now. I'm going to take you home."

"What do you want us to do first, Tom?" Sounds like the sheriff, but I'm not sure.

My father's booming voice shouts, "There are some really big pieces, and maybe we should move those first. John, give me a hand over here. Mike, grab the other end. Carefully. Slowly. Go slow. We don't want to injure him more than he's already injured." They're fighting against the angry ocean. I wish this were all a bad dream, but it isn't. It's a nightmare.

"Now let's form a line and we'll pass the rest of these pieces to a pile over there. It'll go faster that way. We've got to get him out before the tide . . ."

"Pa. Paaaaa. Hurrrr-eeeee." I squeeze my eyes tight until everything turns black.

"We're getting this wood off you, Peter. Just a little more." I can hear them huffing and grunting, and the weight of all the wood on top of me begins to feel lighter. The water washes up over my broken body.

"We've almost got you, Peter. Be careful. Push the seaweed to the side. Get the blankets ready." Pa's definitely in charge.

Now everyone's talking at the same time. Hard to understand what they're saying. So confusing. It's a messy puzzle – a messy . . .

Pa must be furious with me. Bet he thinks I made some bad decisions. I'll tell him I had to find the right wood to carve Ma's birthday present. Then, he won't be mad at me. I could end up with a good wallop on the backside, but that would be better than drowning. It won't hurt too much.

It's good to know Pa's next to me, but the shaking takes over. It's more than the shivers I get when I'm cold. It makes me think of how we shake the apple tree to get the fruit to fall to the ground. I'm shaking so hard, maybe all my teeth will fall out.

"You're just about free, Peter. As soon as we wrap these blankets around you, we'll get you home." Pa's voice is strong, but calm.

"Pa, I didn't give up. I'm not going to die," I whisper.

"You did good, Peter, really good." I close my eyes.

* * *

No surf sounds. The air is warm and . . . that's Ma's soup I smell. "Ooooooh, my head, my eye – they feel like someone is beating on them. I want to touch my eye, but I can't lift my arm. Too weak. Ooooooh." The log walls lap up my moans. All I know is I'm home. I'm safe. The smell of burning wood and the aroma of Ma's homemade vegetable soup make my stomach growl. Yep, I'm home, but I don't remember how I got here. Must have passed out. All I remember is being caged. Stuck. All that wood pinned me to the sand. Thought I would drown. Now, home. Boy, how can I be so lucky?

My brain is rattling around in my skull. A fire rages behind my eyelid. Whatever I did to it can't be good . . . I remember now – something sharp stabbed my eye. I want to open it, but . . . it won't open. "Ma, something's wrong with my eye. Ma, what's going on?"

"Calm down, Peter." Ma's soft calm voice steadies me.

"Ma, I can't open my eye." I wait for an answer, but she's silent. That worries me. I can feel my forehead scrunching up.

"Peter, you'll warm up soon now that you're out of those wet clothes. These warm blankets will help. Pa's got the fire going good and soon you'll think you're out in the sun. The important thing is you're home. You're safe. This is a little warm water to clean up your face, Peter." I hear Ma sipping at the air.

"Don't go near my eye, Ma." A shiver runs from the top of my head down to my soles of my feet.

"I won't Peter, don't worry. I'm just going to wash off the sand and some of this dried blood. I'll be gentle. Try to relax." Ma doesn't sound too upset. Guess it's not as bad as it feels.

My skin responds to the lukewarm damp cloth. Ma's touch is gentle – like she's soothing a baby. I hope she doesn't stop – my stiff body begins to melt. I can feel it. I have to believe it's going to be all right.

"I didn't know you were gone. Where did you go? What were you doing?" Now Ma's voice moves from calm to shaky. That's how she sounds when she's upset. I hate that I caused a lot of headaches – Ma, Pa, the neighbors – I didn't mean for this to happen.

"Be fine, Ma, be fine. Don't worry."

"Your eye is going to be fine, Peter. Dr. Barrett is going to see to it." Ma half mumbles.

I peek out to see her slight figure standing next to Dr. Barrett, who's leaning his tall, heavy body against the wall. He adjusts his black vest.

"I'm really . . . sorry, Ma." My voice cracks.

It's really strange. I don't understand. One minute I know what's happening and then the next, I don't. It's kind of like dreaming, then waking up and then falling back into the dream again.

I can't steady my body parts. My arms and legs jerk all by themselves. Shivers go up my legs into my stomach, then into my chest and finally swirl around my arms. Making matters worse, my brain is empty. Not a thought in it. Can't seem to control anything.

Wish I could open this right eye. It really burns. Must be the salt water. Sand must be in that eye – it's so scratchy. Am I going to see with this eye? I need it to carve. Maybe I won't be able to carve as good as I did before.Maybe not at all. We'll have to wait and see. I'm just happy to be alive. I could've drowned or been eaten by a shark. I should feel happy because I'm alive, but the truth is I want to cry. Tears seep out of my eyes. Can't stop them.

What happened to my wood? I remember clutching it in my right hand. Ma was trying to get it out of my hand. She struggled to pry it loose. I almost died trying to get that stupid piece of wood. I think it fell on the floor, but what happened next is a mystery.

"Let me up. Where's my . . . wood?" My head feels as heavy as the last log I tried to push out of the way, but I'm too weak to get up. My muscles are like mushy hot porridge. When I think of the accident, sweat seeps onto my palms.

The pain comes in waves like a rough sea. The right side of my face is numb. No feeling. My eye thumps as if keeping time with a drum.

Pa's thinking noise, "Hm . . . hm . . . hmmm" buzzes in my ears. God, it's hard to breathe. Feels like a bale of hay sitting on top of me.

Ma's hand squeezes my arm, "Calm down, Peter, you're all right. You're safe now."

Wow, Pa wrinkles his forehead, and the creases are deeper than the rows he plows in the field. He's staring at the doctor.

Dr. Barrett says, "I need to get a good look at that eye. Ann, you did a good job cleaning him up. Now it's my turn."

He must be kidding.

"No, don't touch it," I scream. My fingers tingle.

My words don't matter. Doc's fingers dig like I did looking for treasure under the sand. I yell, "Ouch, stop, it hurts. Get away. I can't . . . . Stop, please stop."

Doc moves away. I squint at him as he removes different instruments from his black bag. I don't like the looks of them. He's not going to get anywhere near my eye with those things. If he thinks . . .

"Let's get a look now, Peter. I'm just going to rinse it with a little clean, warm water. Don't want an infection to start, do you? Come take a look, Tom. You too, Ann," the doctor says.

"Will he lose his sight?" Ma whispers. I hear her question. I shudder not able to control the chill that's going from arms to legs. Doc doesn't answer.

I try to follow the conversation but mostly just squint to look at the dark wood ceiling.

"Stay still, Peter. Try not to move. I'm only going to rinse some of the sand out of your eye with this warm water. It'll sting a little. Give him a sip of brandy, Tom, it'll ease the pain."

What's that taste? Wow, it's strong, but kind of sweet. Makes my lips and tongue warm. It has a strong smell – it's better than that awful cough medicine Ma uses.

"Oooooow, it stings. Oooooow. No more, please." My voice splinters. "Stop, please stop."

"That's all, Peter. I'm finished. You're a good patient. I'm just going to put a little salve on your eye and bandage it to keep it clean. I'm finished for now. Rest," he mutters. As I look at the doc, my good eye plays tricks. First he looks bigger than normal, then he shrinks. Maybe I should just close my eyes.

With my eyes closed, I hear, "Scratches, time . . . wait, patch . . ."

I can't hear everything doc's saying. My thoughts swim through Ma's sniffles. My heart beats in my ears. Jumbled words swim around my head trying to get out, but they're stuck. My head is going to burst.

Strange how my dog is called Patches and now I'll have to wear a patch. I'm really lucky he was with me. So lucky.

He's finished. Thank God, he's finished. No more poking.

"I'll see Peter tomorrow. He has to rest. He's probably going to ache all over. He'll be good when he gets enough rest. Sleep is the best medicine.

"Thank you, Doctor Barrett, Pa says.

"Good night, Mrs. Poppin. Good night, Peter." The wind catches the door behind him, and it slams so hard, the hanging lantern shakes..

I'm stiff like the table under me. My head throbs. If the doctor says I won't be able to see with that eye, I won't believe him. A carver has to have two good eyes to carve beautiful animals.

Heavy air covers my sobs. Patches comes over and puts his head under my hand. I scratch. His tail wags.

"We'll be fine, boy. We'll be fine."

CHAPTER THREE

Where am I? How long have I been asleep? I guess Pa carried me. The sun is up. I'm not used to sleeping late. It's like I got run over by a team of horses – every inch of me is bruised and maybe broken. My eye aches down deep inside, and my head is like a cracked egg. Yep, I'm a mess.

Geez, the shapes and sizes of whatever I look at are not what they should be. Things appear smaller. How strange is that! Nothing's where it should be, a little off to one side. Boy, have I got a problem. If this is how I'm going to see, maybe I won't be able to carve. No, no. That's not going to happen.

I'll wait and see. Ha! That word, 'see' – isn't it silly coming from me whose eye is bandaged. I remember reaching for a piece of wood, falling, wood burying me, being trapped. As if that wasn't bad enough, the incoming tide was about to wash over me. Don't remember much else except the doc working on me. I want to get up, but my legs are like limp seaweed. And . . . I'm dizzy. Yuk, there's that barf feeling.

"Peter, why are you awake? You should rest as much as you can." Ma loves those two words: should and shouldn't. Shouldn't do this. Shouldn't do that. Shouldn't, shouldn't, shouldn't. She's always afraid I'll get hurt and this time, I hate to admit it, she was right. Her voice sounds just as wobbly as my legs.

"I'm sorry Ma, really sorry," I yell from the bed. I really did make a mess of things. I'll get that mermaid carved and make things right.

Pa's head pops through the doorway.

"Good morning, Peter. How does your eye feel?"

With my squinting good eye, I focus on his concerned face. Worry makes him look older than he is. Doesn't look like he got much sleep.

"Sore, Pa, really sore. Can I take this bandage off?"

"Think it needs to stay on. Let's get some food in you."

Pa helps me stand. He holds my arm so tight I couldn't fall even if I wanted to. We inch toward the table.

"Pa, I didn't know Patches was so smart."

"He brought me straight to you, Peter. You're lucky he's your dog," Pa smiles.

"First, eat something," Ma insists.

When she's worried or scared, she always talks about food. She thinks her porridge or soup will fix anything. I have to admit, most of the time it does. The hot porridge, fresh baked brown bread, and homemade raspberry jam fill the empty spaces in my belly. Ma and I picked those raspberries early last summer. Then, she made jam for us and for Pa to sell in the store. I jump when I hear a knock on the door. Must be Doc Barrett. He's going to poke around in my eye again. I don't like it.

"Good morning, Mrs. Poppin."

"Good morning, Doctor." Mom hangs up his coat while he puts his black bag on the empty chair.

"Hello, Peter. You're looking much better today. Must be that jam your Ma's famous for. That'll cure anything that ails you.

"I feel fine, doc. You don't have to check my eye," I have to say it so he'll believe me. No chance.

"Let's take a look at that eye. I hope the swelling's down."

As he loosens the bandage's grip, I shudder.

"I want you to try to open your eye . . . slowly."

I'm as still as a lizard. I don't want to look at him, so with my good eye, I squint at one of my carved wolves on the fireplace mantel. He's actually larger than he looks. Got to find out why things look so small.

"Okay, Peter, open your eye."

I try once, twice. My left eye is now wide open. My right eyelid finally releases its hold on my bottom eyelashes. There it's open.

"But ... but ... I can't see," I scream. My pulse is beating in my ears. My body has this odd trembling rhythm. I know my eye is open, but everything is dark and blurry.

"Ma, I can't see. Pa, I'm . . ." Yellow and white lines swirl around in my head and pick up speed. My muscles quiver just like the leaves on the maple trees when the winter wind chases them to the ground. "I need air." I choke, "Oh God."

"Peter, be still. It's all right." Ma kisses my forehead. I can't look. I close my eyes as tight as I can. "Try to be calm, Peter," Pa says, and then his strong hand squeezes my shoulder. "We want to talk with the doctor for a minute." They walk toward the door.

"Where are you going, Ma?"

"Just out on the porch," she answers. The door slams shut.

I can't hear them, but when they return, Pa stares at the floor. He doesn't look at me. The Doc didn't give them good news, did he?

"Doc says it takes time. We have to wait." Disappointment colors each word. I know that tone. Maybe he thinks my eye can't be saved.

"It's not true, Pa. Don't believe him," I beg. "I'm not really sure, but I don't want you to believe it. I'll see good again. You'll see."

No one answers me.

I'm not satisfied with what the doctor said. I don't want to cry, but tears sneak out of my eyes before I can stop them. My cheeks are wet. My eyes sting like there's seawater in them. How embarrassing. I don't want Pa to see me acting like a baby.

Pa picks up a round black cotton patch with two pieces of braided fabric hanging from each side. He holds it in front of my nose so I'm sure to see it.

"It's too close, Pa." He backs away with his hand still outstretched.

"Peter, you're going to look like a pirate," he says.

"Do I have to?" slips off my tongue. The fact that I don't get an answer is as good as a yes. Well, it might be fun but . . . the older boys will tease me. Don't know what Marian will think.

Pa's stare, as strong and straight as an arrow shoots through me. He turns the patch over and over again. His eyes focus on it. I close my eyes, but I feel Pa's fingers fumbling in my hair trying to get the braids around my head so he can tie them.

"These patches were very important. Some pirates wore them because they had lost or injured an eye. Some wore them for a more important reason. You see, Peter, one or two special pirates worked on deck in the bright sunlight all day; then, the captain would order them to go below decks where it was pitch black."

"How could they see anything in such dark?" I couldn't imagine how that was possible.

"You see, Peter, eyes need time to adjust from daylight to dark. When the pirates went below deck, they would switch the patch to the other eye and the eye that had been hidden on deck . . . could see everything in the dark. When they came outside, they switched the patch back again so the daylight eye was uncovered. A patch is very special."

Pa stared at me, and I stared back wondering if I would ever have to go below decks. I guess Pa told me that so it would make me feel better. I'm not sure it worked. My emotions bump into each other like rocks and shells tossed on the beach. I like the idea of being a special pirate, but I want to see with that eye. My fingers play with the patch.

"Nnnnnnnn, nnnnnnnnnn, nnnnnnnnnn." Patches stares at my patch.

"You don't know what to make of it, do you, boy? It's okay. I'll get used to it. We both will."

His tail thumps against the hard wooden floor.

CHAPTER FOUR

I t's a good day when we're all together for breakfast. Usually, Pa is gone to the field before breakfast is ready. Today he's home because it's a blustery day – gale winds, Pa said. Maybe there's a storm brewing. I like when we're all together at the table.

I've got to talk to him about school, and I have to tell him about the men on the bluff.

"I don't . . . I don't want to go to school," My tone makes my folks look up. "Not with *this* patch. I'll wear it when I come home." With my finger, I trace the circular black patch covering my eye.

Pa makes a little noise in his throat like he wants to say something. He does that at his meetings.

"You must do two things today," he finally says firmly. His jaw muscles move because he's grinding his teeth together.

"Wear the patch and go to school."

I can't look at my father. I turn away.

"Ma, do I *have to* go?" I beg.

"Yes, you heard right. School for you, Peter, and that's that. Don't be asking your mother. She agrees with me. You've missed enough learning. You don't want to be at the bottom of your class. Do you?"

Nothing I can say will change his mind. That's for sure. Well, in that case, I'll tell everyone the story, and they'll all want a patch, or I'll tell them a pirate gave it to me, and they'll want me to get one for them. In any case, I'll call it a badge of courage. That'll work, won't it?

What's good about school anyway? Well, there's always Miss Prim. One day in town, I saw her hair down, not in the bun like she usually wears. When the sun hit it, it was like spun gold. She pulls it back tight to make herself look stern. But she's really not. She's warm and sweet like wildflower honey. Her voice is just as soft as lamb's wool.

I know she likes me. I finish all my work, and my answers are always correct. The older kids hate that. They call me her favorite. Me and . . . Marian. Well, maybe we are, but you won't hear us complaining.

"The kids are going to tease me. They'll call me names. Maybe they'll call me Patches, just like my dog." When Pa hears that, he looks over at me but remains silent.

I'll try the cramp trick. I bend over. My hair almost touches the wood planks.

"I don't feel good, Ma. Think I'm going to be sick."

"Peter, if you think you're going to stay home, you're dreaming. Now get your book and get."

Her mind is set. Pa's still silent. No one is going to give in.

The still early morning air is sliced by the school bell. Darn, I'm late. I grab my book, stomp out the door with Patches trailing behind.

"You can't go with me, boy."

"Ahruuf, ruuf." I lean down, my fingers find that favorite spot on his back and give it a good scratch. "There's nothing at school you'd like, boy. You stay here." I point my index finger straight down and Patches lies down.

"You stay. Good boy."

I haven't gone far when my eye starts to throb. School will be awful.

I'll take this path. It's the fastest way to get to school. The maple trees are red, orange, and gold while the spruces and pines are shades of green. I love when the leaves fall. They crunch under my feet, and the pieces become smaller and smaller until they're almost dust.

* * *

Good, the doors are still open. If I creep up these steps and slip inside, nobody will notice. Maybe I can . . .

"Look, it's Peter," cries Jenny. Heads turn. Fifteen pair of owl eyes stare at me. They're really staring at my patch. Then it happens.

First, one laugh, then a chorus.

"Stop laughing," I shriek.

"Peter wants to be a pirate," Jacob yells. Laughter fills the schoolroom. It's just like I thought it would be and I've only been in school five minutes. I've got to get out of here, but I can't. I'm frozen in place staring past the bobbing heads straight at my teacher.

"Boys and girls stop it," demands Miss Prim, who is quick getting to my side. She, too, stares down at the black circle covering my eye. My chin finds my chest. Did anyone tell her about my accident, my eye or that I'd come back to school wearing this patch?

"Peter, come take my chair. It's all right." I wobble forward.

I hear them. Jacob and his friends, in the back of the room, they whisper and snicker. Miss Prim inhales so much air you'd think she'd pop like a balloon. She shoots a piercing arrow stare at the back of the room. The boys stop.

"Can I go home, Ma'am? Please," I plead.

Miss Prim's pretty head moves side to side. I'm going to throw up.

Marian, with pigtails the color of coal, smiles gently at me. My heart gallops.

"Oh Peter, it's too awful. I'm so sorry your eye is . . ."

"Wimp," a voice in the back of the room utters almost too soft to be heard, but I heard it and so did Miss Prim.

"Who said that?" she barks. Her words crumble the quiet.

"Peter was seriously hurt, and I don't want anyone behaving badly. That comment is not acceptable. I won't tolerate it."

Miss Prim's voice rattles the windows. We've never heard her angry voice. Heads bow, eyeballs blink at the wooden desks. Marian's tears drip onto the slate in front of her. She looks up. Her eyes crash into mine.

"We're glad you're here and that you're all right," Miss Prim says with her restored angel voice. The corners of her mouth are pulled back ever so gently.

I think I love her. I do. I do. I glance up. My eyes land on a wooden cross on the church's back wall. In front of God, I've declared my love for Miss Prim. I wonder if it's okay.

School is over. My eye aches while a lump forms in my throat. I just want to leave. By the time I get outside, the older boys, who stick together, are huddled under the old elm. I can't tell who's there. They're hidden in the shade. The others run out the gate anxious to get home. I wish someone stayed behind.

"Peeeeeter, Peeeeeeter, Peter is a pansy." One begins the chant, and they all join the chorus.

"Whiner, whiner, wimpy whiner," yells Joel, who's taller than Pa's horse.

He's always in touble picking fights with me or someone else. Pa says he's jealous that I'm smart. He can't leave me alone. He's such a pain.

"You just want the girls to feel sorry for you." The untrue words fly at me like rotten apples. "There's nothing wrong with your eye. You're pretending. You want people to think you're hurt. That's why you have the patch." The words sting.

"I am *not* pretending. I'll show you my eye." There's a knot. Can't get this untied. Suddenly, Teddy Talmidge grabs me from behind. I'm down.

"Get off me. Stop it. Stop. Leave me alone," I bellow. The sound I make reminds me of a moose.

Everyone's gone. Got to handle this myself. Not going to be easy - six against one. Got to get him off me. He's heavy just like the logs. Got to keep my eye covered.

"Peter Patch," someone cries.

"Peter Poppin Patch. That's it. That's your new name." Over and over their words bounce around me.

"Peter Poppin Patch. Peter Poppin Patch. Sissy, sissy. Why don't you fight us?" I hate them all. I cover my ears, but I hear every word. If I can get to my feet . . .

"Pansy, pansy – Peter Poppin." I spin around trying to find a target. My arms sweep left and right. "I'll get you," I yell out. Now I wish Patches was here.

Out of nowhere a swoosh - the sound of giant beating wings. What's that? I squint toward the sky.

"Eeeeeee. Eeeeeeee." A shrieking cry. "Eeeeeeee. Eeeeeeee."

The untamed sound fills the air in a deafening way. The boys scream and scatter.

"Run, Peter, run." The eagle's command pours into me.

An eagle – it's an eagle. It's the most magnificent eagle I've ever seen. He circles and dives over and over. He's . . . defending me. His enormous wings brush the boys' heads. The sun hits his wings, and they glimmer. He's not like other eagles. He's . . . my eagle.

They're all running and screaming. Is this really happening?

My eye burns, but I have to run. Must follow the eagle. I can't stop. I've got to hold this patch against my eye.

"Run, run. I must run," I scream outloud until my voice cracks.

I have to get home. Run! I've got to run. Can't stop. Where's the cabin? Can't see it. There it is. I'm safe. Patches is sleeping on the porch.

"Oh Patches, you don't know what happened today. I needed you." He tilts his head to one side and then barks, as if to say, 'yes, I know.'

I push the door open. It bangs against the wall.

"Ma, Ma . . . the boys . . ." I struggle to get air in my lungs.

Before I can take another step, the floor comes up to meet me. I squint at Ma's old worn shoes. My body doesn't want to stand.

"Ma, it was awful . . . but it was incredible too." I struggle to my feet, and the words find their way out of my mouth.

"An eagle, a giant shimmery eagle with wings as big as our wagon saved me. It swooped down. The boys ran. Ma, it told me to run."

"Peter, slow down. I don't understand. Calm yourself. What's this about an eagle?"

I don't have enough air to explain everything. I teeter from side to side. Ma's arms whip around me. Does she think I made it up? She's got to understand.

"Ma, please listen. Over and over, the bullies chanted, 'Peter Pansy – Peter Poppin Pansy'. They jumped on me. The eagle dove at them again and again. The eagle wanted to save me. He kept circling – protecting me. The eagle's cries kept telling me to run. Ma, you should've seen this eagle. So beautiful. I was scared, Ma, really terrified."

"How did the eagle know he was to protect you? It's very confusing. You've been through so much. First, the accident and now bullies . . . and an eagle. It's just too much."

Her forehead wrinkles. "Peter, you're soaking wet. Your patch is full of sweat. I'll wash it." She reaches behind my head and unties the knot. The sweaty patch dangles between us.

She stares at my eye. "Oh, Peter," she snaps at the air. "Your eye is black and blue like you were in a fist fight. I didn't realize how . . ."

"Ma, please listen. My eye will be all right. Did you hear what I said about the eagle?"

"Peter, you'll have to tell your father everything. He'll know what to make of it. Do you know why the eagle came to you?"

"No, Ma, but I know he was protecting me." My racing heart bounces off my ribs. Hope they don't break. I straighten up, pull my shoulders back and with a solemn look and a lower voice and say, "Ma, I won't go back to school."

"Of course you ..."

"No, Ma, I won't. You can't make me. I can't. I'm not going back."

We stare at each other. Who's going to speak first? She starts to reach for a towel but changes her mind. Her sticky wet hands circle around me so fast I can't step back. I want to pull away, but she holds tight. The only thought floating in my head is that my Ma cares, she really cares. Tears dot her apron.

CHAPTER FIVE

What a racket! Those noisy blackbirds outside my window could wake a bear from hibernation. Their high pitch squaks remind me of the old wagon. I'm too comfortable under these covers to get up. If I don't get up, if I pretend to be asleep, maybe they'll let me stay home.

I hear Pa in the kitchen. His voice is much louder than I'm used to. Bet he's talking to Ma about the bullying. He won't let those boys get away with that. But . . . if Pa fights my battles for me, those kids will think I'm weak. They'll call me a Papa's boy or worse. I've got to solve my own problems.

Why aren't they calling me to breakfast? I'd better get up. Maybe . . .

Ma appears in the doorway. Her teeth scrape her lower lip until I can't see them. Not a good sign. I want to talk to her about school, about the older boys, about my eye, but the way she's staring at me pushes the words back down my throat.

"Good morning, Peter." Ma sounds like nothing's happened, but her look tells me differently. "I have your breakfast. Are you hungry?"

"Ah, huh. Ma, why didn't you call me for school? Is Pa still here?"

"No, Peter, he left." Before I can ask another question, she disappears into the kitchen. I'm two steps behind her.

"Where's Patches, Ma?"

"He took Patches with him to the field."

"Dr. Barrett says you must rest. You were very troubled yesterday, and we don't want you to be under more pressure, so you'll stay home today. That's good news. Pa went to talk to Miss Prim. He wants the teasing and bullying to stop and the cruel boys to be punished."

"Ma, I don't want Pa to fight my battles for me. I can take care of myself. I just didn't expect what happened, and it surprised me. The truth is I'm all right now."

I wonder if my mother hears how brave I think I am. But am I? I want to take care of my own problems, but I'm not sure I know how. Which is best – Pa talking to Miss Prim or not talking to her? If anyone sees him, they'll call me a pansy again. I just know it. Which is worse – name calling or bullying? What awful choices.

I remember when Jessie hid my book outside behind the church and Pa went to school and complained. Another time someone took my slate. As soon as Pa heard about it, he wanted to jump in, but I told him I had just misplaced it. That was a lie.

Ma's lips part and words creep out, "Peter, the night of your accident when the doctor examined your eye, you were holding something. It fell under the table. When I found it, I put it in the corner cupboard."

Ma's damp hands smooth out her apron as she walks to the cupboard. As she opens the door, she asks, "Were you going to carve something? This looks like a fine piece of wood."

"I was thinking about it." She stares at me waiting for me to tell her what my plans were.

I change the subject. "Ma, these are the best pancakes ever." She won't ask any more questions if I talk about her cooking. She smiles broadly, leans down and kisses the top of my head.

I stare at the treasured wood she put on the table – the ideal driftwood – the wood I almost lost my life for. It's as white as the Sweet White Violets that blanket the fields in the spring. I see its curves and its beautiful grain even with one eye. Boy, when I think of that wood, everything comes back like a wild river flooding its banks. It was a challenge to reach this wood. But, I got it.

"Thanks, Ma. This is a good piece." I want to say 'special', but I don't want her to know how special it is or what I aim to do with it. It has to be a surprise. I still have a month till her birthday.

"You really had to have that piece, didn't you? You just about lost your life getting it. Maybe it would be good if you worked on it today.

Go on, Peter, finish your breakfast and get out to the shed where you can figure out what to do with it."

Ma's grin brings back good memories of carving so I smile back. The more I think about working with that wood, the stronger I feel. I only hope that I can see well enough to carve. I can only see flashes of light with that eye. I'll just have to see how it goes.

"Take a jacket, Peter. The shed is freezing. No one's been in there for weeks. How about a hug." Ma's hugs always warm me up. They're strong medicine for what ails me. Enough about hugs, there's work to be done. The door slams behind me.

"Sorry, Ma."

*   *   *

"Hey, doggie, are you going to keep me company while I work in the shed?" Already he's at the door waiting.

Ma's right. It's biting cold in here. Better start a fire. A little straw, a few pieces of kindling and one or two pieces of that dry brittle oak should do it. Hope these old matches will light. That's better. Even a little fire puts out a lot of heat.

"It'll warn up soon enough. You'd better stay near the stove, doggie." I watch as he circles twice before curing up in front of the stove.

I'll need this chisel, a small mallet, a sharpening stone and my favorite knife. They're all important for this carving. Here by the window, I'll have enough light to get started.

On paper, my sketch of the mermaid is exactly like what I've imagined a million times. Even if my eyes are closed, every detail is clear. Ma loved the carving on that ship we saw in the harbor. I remember how she talked about its glorious tail. A couple of times, she's hinted that I should carve one. This piece is long enough for that unique tail. Ma is going to have her mermaid.

Everything about this wood is perfect even its bumps. Its thickness and texture are practically in the right places. I've got to handle this wood as if it's destined to be on the bow of a schooner.

Hey, what the . . .?

I thought I put my finger on this dark spot, but I'm not on it. Maybe it's because I can see with only one eye? What I see is very different. Wow, if I keep my head straight, I can't see anything on my right side and . . . it's like I don't know how far the table is from my finger when I point at it. How will I be able to carve? Don't really know but I have to try. I'll practice on a piece of scrap beech wood first.

No. That's too deep. That's not deep enough - that's not right. What's going on? My voice gets louder. Patches senses something is wrong. He trots over and rests his head in my lap.

"Yes, boy, I'm upset. I can't control my tools. Can't carve. It's hopeless." I push my friend away. "Go lie down. Leave me alone."

Why can't I hold the tools right? This knife feels like a stranger in my palm. Sould feel like I'm shaking hands with an old friend. It's hard to wrap my fingers around it. My hands are a mess. I didn't realize how banged up they got. I was trying to stop all that wood from falling on me. I couldn't stop it all. That's what all these cuts and bruises are from. They're almost healed. I don't understand. My fingers are so stiff. It's awkward. I feel like I've never carved before. If I hold it at a different angle and cut this way, maybe it'll work.

Okay, I'll make a cut here.

"Ouch. Cut the wood, stupid, not your hand." I hear my voice bounce off the shed's walls. I've given myself a deep cut. I've got a big piece of skin hanging loose. Blood drips all over everything. What a mess! Where's that bucket of water? Wow, it's really deep almost to the bone.

"Why can't I carve? Maybe I'm finished as a carver," I scream loud enough to interrupt anyone who's having a quiet dinner. I don't care, and I don't need any of these.

Bam! Crash!

Tools fly through the air and bounce off the walls slamming into anything in their way. Patches hides in the corner. The mallet strikes a window and tears a hole in the brittle covering. I stare at the hole, not feeling the least bit sorry.

"I don't care. I don't want . . . no, I don't need any of these tools. I don't care if I carve."

Ma's figure comes flying through the door.

"Peter, are you all right? What's going on? What was that noise? How can you see anything? I realize we're standing in the dark. Ma lights the oil lamp. She gasps.

I'm bleeding, tools are all over on the floor, there a hole in the window covering and Ma's lighting the old oil lamp. Doesn't make sense.

"You're bleeding. Let me see your hand. We've got to clean this. Are you cut any place else? Peter, I'm talking to you. Say something."

I'm glad she wants to know if I'm hurt. I want to tell her it's nothing, but I don't. The words are locked somewhere behind my lips. I just stand there with blood dripping off the tip of my fingers onto the floor.

All I want to do is disappear. I slam the door leaving my mother in the mess. Daylight's almost gone. The sky is pink then purple. It looks like the clouds are in just the right place to reflect the western light. It's so beautiful. I wish I could capture that sky. Makes me feel calm.

Hey, who's up on our bluff? I'd recognize that hat anywhere. How could I forget an outfit like that? Those are the two men who were watching me when I was trapped. I wonder what they're doing here? This is the second time I've seen them on our property. I forgot to tell Pa about them. I'll do it tonight as soon as he comes home. Right now I need to take care of my hand. I'll wash it off out here instead of making more of a mess inside. Ouch - that stings. Got to stop this bleeding.

I don't know what got into me. I made a complete mess in the shed. I hope my wood is okay. I probably should clean up the tools and the blood. Suddenly, I look up into Ma's face. Angry, but . . . there's worry too. Her fingers are rolled into her palms. They make tight balls. What can I say?

"Let's rinse off some of that blood. I need to see how deep that cut is."

"Ma, I'll clean up the shed," I offer, watching her chew the inside of her cheek. She's still breathing hard.

I look into her sad eyes. "I don't blame you for being angry. I didn't mean to yell and throw things around. I don't know why I did it." Her look softens, and she tucks a loose strand of hair behind her ear. Good, no more fists.

"You sure did scare Patches. He's still in the corner. Be there for a while, I guess. You were disappointed and angry, Peter. Do you feel better after throwing everything around?" She takes a step toward me.

"Yes, ma'am." Ma takes my hand and inspects the cut making sure it's clean. I grimace when she pulls the skin back, but I don't make a sound.

"This isn't as bad as I thought," she says. I'll just lather a bit of this ointment on it. It doesn't smell, and it won't sting." She winds the cotton bandage around and around. My bandaged hand looks a lot more serious than the cut actually is. It's just one more thing to add to a miserable day. I look up into her anxious expression. She almost smiles but decides a sigh is better.

When the door swings open, Pa's smile announces that his day went well.

"Ann, Peter, Miss Prim says bullying won't happen again. If it does, there will be consequences. The bullies won't be able to attend school."

I knew it. He took care of my problem. I don't know if I should be happy or sad. Again, I didn't solve my own problem, Pa did. I'm getting too old to have Pa stick up for me. I've got to talk to him. He'll understand.

Ma and Pa sit opposite each other. Ma's eyes along with her wrinkled forehead announce her concern.

"School is not Peter's only problem, Tom. He tried to carve today, and it was a disaster. There's a mess in the shed, and he even cut himself. You know how important whittling is to him."

Pa turns to face me and asks matter-of-factly, "What's going on? Peter, why couldn't you carve? You're very skilled." My father's words paint me as an experienced wood carver. Maybe I once was, but it's not true any more.

Pa reaches across the table and Ma's hands disappear inside his. She sighs, "That's true, but . . . that was before he lost the use of his eye and before he spent days without carving. He can't see, and he can't feel, and I have no idea how to help him. He says things aren't where he thinks they are. It must be because he's looking with one eye." Ma's head jerks left, right, left, right. She doesn't know what to do.

"It's just that he has to develop new skills. Right, Peter?" My father tries to sound confident that it can and will happen. I can't look him in the eye.

Suddenly, an aroma fills the warm cabin air. Ma's venison stew smell tickles my nose. Homemade brown bread takes its place on a wooden plank waiting to be sliced. We stretch out our arms, take hold of a warm hand, bow our heads and say our thanks.

"Thank you, Lord, for our food, our family and the successes of today." When Pa is finished, I add, "Thank you, God, for my one good eye and my parents. Amen." We eat in silence. Pa finally breaks the stillness.

"Were you disappointed not being able to carve today, Peter?" His eyes shift from his plate to my eye. I plow my potatoes around my plate. "With time, your one perfect eye will do the work of two, and your fingers will be retrained. Remember how we had to teach our horse, Tilly, to walk again after she broke her leg?"

My muted voice answers, "Yeah, Pa. I remember."

"She did it, didn't she, Peter? Now she's as good as new." I'm immobile remembering poor Tilly and the hours of work she had to do before she could walk. The one clear picture in my mind is Tilly, struggling to walk. It was sad to watch.

Pa stands up and shuffles slowly to the fireplace.

"Come sit with me, Peter. I want to talk to you." Ma disappears. When Pa wants to talk to me alone, she calls this 'men talk.' Now I'll have a chance to tell Pa about the men and the mermaid. We get comfortable in the rocking chairs by the fire. Patches curls up by my feet. He looks calm now – wish I was.

"Pa, there's something I meant to tell you before, but I forgot. There are two men – really strange looking. Odd hat, long coats, heavy beards – kind of old. They were on the bluff the day the pile of driftwood fell on me. I think they saw the whole thing."

"They didn't come to help you?" I can tell his mood is changing.

"No, Pa. I called, but they didn't answer. I don't think they could hear me. Too much wind. Well, they were walking along the bluff tonight. I saw them when I was rinsing the blood off my hand at the pump."

"I can't believe they didn't help you. You could've drowned." The look that crosses Pa's face tells me he's angry. "Wonder what they're doing here?" Pa rubs his chin and his eyelids flicker which means he's trying to figure something out. "I'll ask around in town and see if anyone knows about them."

"About your carving, son, it takes time . . ." Pa's eyes soften. He knows how important it is to me and he's as concerned as I am about my eyesight.

"I know Pa. But I want you to know why I got so upset. I'm trying to carve a mermaid for Ma's birthday, and I don't have a lot of time. It's really important."

"I see. Now I understand why you're so frustrated." Pa's long arms bridge the space between us. His over-sized hands pat my shoulders, "That's good, really good, son."

I aim to let Pa know why this carving is so important. "A mermaid is Ma's favorite. She saw a mermaid figurehead on a ship in the harbor. Mr. Jamieson, who runs the mill, worked on the docks back in England. He told me stories about figureheads. Carvers made all kinds: warriors and eagles, but the mermaid was their favorite. I remember I asked him why they like her so much. He said the sailors believed her beauty would calm an angry sea, and guard the ships from sickness, rocks, storms and dangerous winds. I figured if I made one for Ma, it would keep everyone in our house safe."

"That's a pretty important project, Peter. I'm sure you'll find a way to get it done. If you need my help, just ask me." I feel relieved. Pa knows about the men, and he knows what I'm trying to do for Ma. My chest lets go. I close my eyes. I'm ready for bed.

"So... it'll be school tomorrow," Pa says and then waits. I don't answer. That's not exactly what I wanted to hear.

"May I be excused, Pa? My thoughts fly to school and the troubles I had with being teased. I try to chase the memory away by scrunching my eyes shut, but it doesn't work. Image still there.

"Sleep well, Peter." Pa's weary voice trails after me. I walk in a straight line across the room.

"Come on, Patches." He brushes past me and sits beside my bed. I look over my shoulder into my father's stare.

"Thanks, Pa."

CHAPTER SIX

"Peter, time to get up. Peter, did you hear me?"

My good eye squints at the window. It's dark outside. The sun isn't up.

"Peter, you'll be late if you don't get going."

My eyes move from the dark window to the doorway. I can't see Ma's face. The light behind her paints her as a dark figure with a light outline around her. But I can see enough to know that her fingers are rolled up into balls and these rest on her hips. Her voice tells me she's not smiling. I inch Ma's hand-made quilt from my body and a shiver travels from my head into my feet jittering on the ice-cold wooden planks.

"Why do I have to get up so early, Ma?'

"You're going to school today. Remember? And . . . Pa needs your help before breakfast. Get up." I look around for Patches, but he's not there. If I'm going to school, maybe I can figure out a way to take him with me.

The thought of school makes me want to throw up! I know an education is important to Pa, but I'd rather help him in the store. I'd even shovel out Tilly's stall. Maybe I should try to carve. Nah, not going to happen. School is where I'll be.

"Peter?"

"I'm up, Ma. Where's Pa? Where's Patches?"

"Patches is outside with Pa. They're waiting for you. Better wear a jacket – sun hasn't warmed the air."

* * *

"I'm here, Pa. What do you need me to do? Boy, it's cold. Gotta keep moving.

"Come here, boy." I rub his head and his tail goes wild. He's always happy to see me.

"Peter, I need to move these sacks of grain. Can't do it alone. My back isn't good today. Grab the other side, son."

"Pa, did you work in the field yesterday? I bet you lifted something heavy. Wish I could lift these sacks by myself, but I'm not that strong, yet." I move closer but all I hear is Pa's heavy labored breathing.

The cabin door opens. Ma's voice is as crisp as the air, "Breakfast is ready."

The last sack is stacked in the shed.

"Thanks, son." The heavy wooden door creaks open, and the warm air colored by Ma's baking bread fills my nose and teases my stomach.

"I'm ready for three bowls of porridge, Ma, and I think Patches is ready too. Look how that tail is wagging. He knows it's breakfast time."

* * *

Warm milk and honey on this porridge will heat my chilled innards. I look at Pa and wonder about his trip to school. What did he and Miss Prim talk about? I know he believed her when she said there wouldn't be more teasing. The bullies won't be calling me names. I hope not.

Besides, I want to see Josh and Phillip and find out if they've gone hunting. Will I be able to hunt using one eye? I'll have to wait and see.

The other person I really want to see is Marian. She's really pretty. Her cheeks are always pink and most of the time, she smiles when she sees me. Sometimes when she looks at me, it's hard to see her eyes under all those eyelashes. She has enough for two people. I like when she tosses her head from one side to the other. Her curls bounce up and down.

We grew up together. Attended the same one-room school up north. I was pretty excited when Pa told me her family would move with us to settle this town. Josh and Phillip, my hunting friends are fun, but they're not Marian. She's got brains. She can do the hardest arithmetic problems. She always finishes first. Besides, she speaks French. I never met anyone who spoke another language. Wait a minute. I do know someone. The Indian boy who's new this year. He pretty much stays to himself. Real quiet. Doesn't volunteer a lot like most of us do, but when he answers Miss Prim, his English is good. He speaks his native language, Abamela, and English. I wish I could speak another language. I'm going to learn some Abamela language, and if Marian teaches me a few French words, I'll know three languages.

One time Miss Prim asked Marian how to say a word in French. When she said it, it was like music. Then we all tried to say the word, and it didn't sound the same. We couldn't stop laughing.

I wanted Marian to go with me to look for wood, but she wasn't in school. If I knew the Indian boy better, I could have asked him. He could have gotten me out from under that wood-stack. Instead, it was my dog that went with me and he's the one who really saved me. He got Pa.

* * *

I'll be at school early. I'm walking better today. A lot of aches and pains are gone. All that work I did with Pa this morning must have warmed up my muscles. The schoolyard is almost empty, but I see just what I don't need. Jacob and Tommy. I don't want to deal with bullies today. Can I get by them without their saying anything? I could turn back. Nope, that won't work. Ma would only send me back. If I look the other way . . . Great, not even a whisper. They didn't even look my way. That was easy.

Clang.

Clang.

Clang.

I swear that bell gets louder every time Miss Prim rings it. You can hear it even if you're miles away. Bet they can hear it in the Indian village. There's Marian. Like always, she's early. I like how she waits at the top of the steps.

"Hi, Marian. Thanks for waiting for me."

"Hi, Peter. I'm glad to see you, but how did you know I was waiting for you?" She flutters her eyelashes and a tiny smile flashes at me. She raises her right eyebrow. It's neat how she can move one eyebrow and then the other. I can't do that. "Will you teach me how to move my eyebrows like you do?" I wink. She blushes.

"I just guessed." Marian's grin lets me know that was the right answer. I want to tell her about my disaster with carving, but . . .

"Peter what happened to your hand?" My friend's blue eyes flash her inner concern. Her hand covers her mouth. Then she stutters, "Oh Peter . . . first your eye, now your hand. What's next?"

"Marian, do you remember when we were young how I was always tripping and falling? I must have cut my knees and shins a million times." I lower my head remembering all the bruises I had.

"Of course I remember. When you fell, I would run and get water and pour it on your scrapes and cuts. You've always been clumsy." She pulls herself up to her full height, raises her chin. She looks like she thinks she's better than I am.

"I'm not that clumsy," I say in a tone that shows my hurt pride. "But maybe it's no wonder I had that accident on the beach. Funny thing is I don't remember you ever falling." I feel a strange feeling in my throat. I look away not wanting to have her eyes meet mine.

"Peter, what's the matter? Are you all right? I asked you about your hand. Did you hear me?"

"It's just a cut, Marian, nothing serious. I'll tell you about it later. Right now, I need to tell you something important." I'm about to go on when she interrupts.

"What is it, Peter. Tell me."

"I'm trying. Wait a minute." She twists her head around and scowls at me.

"Sorry, Marian. Well, it's like this . . . To carve well, I've got to be able to see with both eyes, not just one. My work won't be any good if I don't see with both eyes." My lips won't let the other words leave my mouth when my friend's expression tells me to stop. Her clear eyes are turning into a deep pool of tears. I don't want her to cry. "Don't worry, Marian, Pa told me I can retrain my one eye so it sees like two. Our horse, Tilly, had to learn how to walk after her accident, and she did. So I can teach my right eye to see like two. It'll take time, but I can do it."

"What are you talking about?" Her nose wrinkles and her curls shake. It's time to change the subject. I look past Marian trying to concentrate on the steps behind her.

"Never mind. Let's talk about something else."

She stares for a moment, then, blinks. "All right, Peter, if that's . . ." Very slowly she samples the air. She exhales slowly. The corners of her mouth pull back while a tiny blush tints her cheeks. I feel the tight lines on my face soften as I breathe her calm air. I know Marian would like me to talk about everything, but I can't.

Clang, Clang, Clang. The second bell.

I'm glad I don't have to walk into the schoolroom alone. It's a good feeling having Marian next to me. My body shivers in the cold. One pot-bellied stove to heat this room is not enough. The room is about twenty feet wide and double that from the front door to the back wall. It'll take a while.

Our benches and tables not too far from the stove in the corner. Miss Prim's desk is close to the heat. That's a good thing. She always wears two heavy crocheted shawls. When all the students are here, the room warms up faster. Must be all that body heat. Today, there's a deep chill. I start wondering who is absent.

I pull my jacket tighter around me. I feel something in my pocket and think of the fabric-covered bundle I dug out of the sand. It's the - my special box. I finger it. My index fingers get that prickly feeling – like it has pins and needles. By the end of the day, I'm ready to tell Marian everything.

* * *

"Marian, let's sit under the oak. I don't want anyone to hear what I'm saying, it's only for your ears." The old oak stood a short distance from us. Any time someone wanted to talk about something without everyone hearing, they would go to the old oak. If it could speak, it would have lots of secrets to tell, I'm sure of it.

I sample the dry air, glance at Marian whose eyes focus on my mouth. I can't wait any longer. I've got to tell her.

"Marian, before the wood fell on me, I was digging in the sand ..."

"Whatever for? Did you think you'd find a treasure?" I don't find what she said funny. I don't say anything. It's better to just go on. When someone makes that kind of a comment, it's best just to go on and ignore it.

"I'm not sure, but I found something . . . something special."

"Is it here? Show it to me. I want to see it. I want to see this *treasure*." Marian's excitement surprises me.

"We don't have a lot of time before we both have to start for home." I try to put her off, but she pulls herself up to her full height, folds her arms across her chest and squints through her long dark lashes.

"If I can't see it right now, maybe I won't want to see it later." Of course, she'll want to see it, but her curiosity is galloping away with her. She doesn't like secrets, and she's not very patient. I guess it's my fault that she wants to see it now. If I didn't want to show her, then I shouldn't have talked about it.

"Okay, okay. Don't be like that. I'll show you." My fingers fumble with the odd-wrapped object. I pull it out of my pocket and unfurl my fingers. I spread my fingers so it doesn't fall off my hand. I slowly lift my head to see Marian's reaction.

"Yuk, that's it? What is it? It stinks like seaweed. Why are you carrying it around in your pocket?" Is that all she can say?

"Marian, listen. Just listen. First, I dug up shells and rocks covered with barnacles. Then, I brought up this box – it could be silver." I peel back the old falling-apart blue cloth.

"I know it doesn't look like anything special. Look how clean it is in spots. I can't figure it out. The weird part is what happens when I hold it. My fingers don't want to put it down, and they tingle. It's like not being able to let go. It must have some power."

Marian opens and closes her eyelids a hundred times. "Don't be silly, Peter. It's just an old box. I can't believe you think it has a special power. That's ridiculous." I know she doesn't believe me.

"You're not hearing me, Marian. I can't believe you think it's only an old box. You're wrong. I know it's something special. Sometimes . . . sometimes . . . Marian, every word I've told you is true. If you don't believe me, how will the others believe me? Ugh! This is one of those times when you're hard to talk to and I don't want to waste my time."

Marian is rooted to the spot. Her head sinks forward. Her chin lands on her chest. Her frame crumbles. Instantly, I feel sick to my stomach. It's just that I need her to believe me. I shouldn't have been so hard on her.

"I'm sorry, Marian, but I need you more than anyone to believe me." I inch toward her. She takes a step back. She stares and for a moment, there's silence.

"I do believe you, Peter. It's just so un . . . unusual and unfamiliar. I'm your true friend, and we'll be friends forever." I feel a smile trying to form on my lips, but my nerves jiggle inside and the smile disappears.

I've got to get home now, Peter, but you really need to show me that box – and tell me everything."

"I will show you, Marian. I promise. We'll have more time to talk tomorrow and . . . See you tomorrow. Bye."

I turn away. I don't wave. The walk home seems to take longer because my brain is trying to sort out everything that just happened. I feel confused. I don't understand most of it.

* * *

Another school day and all I can hope for is one like yesterday without anyone teasing me. The steps are empty. My heart sinks. I go into the cold room. I spot Marian. There's an empty seat two rows behind her.

"Ah-hem." I cough trying to get her to turn around. No luck. I guess she's mad at me about yesterday. I can't worry about that now, but I do wish she would turn around and say hello. She doesn't. That's okay. Miss Prim won't be happy if I don't pay attention to the lesson anyway.

I decide it'll be good if I get to know the Indian boy. I take a quick look around the room and see where he's sitting. He notices that I'm looking at him, but he looks down. Maybe he doesn't understand that if I'm looking at him, it means I want to talk to him.

"Peter, did you hear the question?" Miss Prim is moving quickly in my direction. "Peter, what are you doing?"

"Nothing, Miss Prim, I was . . ." When I look past my teacher, I see Marian. She turns around and . . . surprises me with a smile. That's a good sign, or is she just happy that I got in trouble.

"Peter," Miss Prim, whispers, "Be here with the lesson. Not outside or anywhere else."

"Yes, ma'am."

"Go outside now, children. I'll ring the bell when it's time for you to come in."

"Peter, do you want to play with us?" Tommy is at the door waiting for me.

"I wish I could play with you guys at recess, but when I run, pain shoots up the back of my head." I hate being the only one who can't run around.

I spot the Indian boy standing next to the gate. He's alone. His foot kicks at the dirt. I don't know anything about him. Maybe it's time for me to make a new friend. I've heard him answer Miss Prim in English, so I think he'll understand me. His English isn't perfect, but he understands enough. Anyway, my English isn't perfect either.

"Hi, I'm Peter. I touch my chest with my hand. Then pointing at him I ask, "What's your name?" His forehead wrinkles a little while his eyes narrow.

"Ahmik." Without hesitating, he says his name again, "I'm Ahmik." He stares at me. I'm not sure how much he understands, but I guess I'll find out. I smile and jerk my head toward the old tree.

"Let's sit there." I hope he'll follow me. He does.

I've never been this close to him in class, and if I was, I didn't notice how tall he is. He looks like he could be older too. His dark reddish brown skin is like rusted metal. His hair is dark, much darker than Marian's. It brushes against his shoulders. We don't look alike. Me with green eyes and blonde hair and . . . well, his eyes . . . they're black like his hair. It's strange how he's been in my class, but I just didn't take notice. Even though our class is small, we have different ages. The youngest girl is five and the oldest boy is sixteen. The only students I really know are the few who are about my age and whose parents know my Pa and do business in his store.

"How old are you," I ask. He hesitates then says quietly, "Fourteen."

"I'm thirteen," I say. It's good that we're close in age. Right away I get that special feeling. The kind I get when I know someone will be a good friend.

"Maybe we can study together," I say.

"I teach you how hunt with bow," my new friend says. This is good.

I pick a clear spot and get comfortable on the ground. Ahmik waits until I'm settled, then sits cross-legged about two feet from me. His eyes scan the dirt as if he's searching for words. I clear my throat. His head bobs up. His deep-set eyes zero in on the black fabric patch concealing my eye.

Before I can say anything, he asks, "What happen to eye?" I lift the patch enough to make my injured eye visible.

"A stick jabbed me in the eye." His stare gets wider. I reach for a stick on the ground and poke the palm of my hand. "Jab, jab, jab," I say stabbing my hand. Then I touch my patch. He scrunches his eyes shut and his head moves a little to the left and then the right.

"Your eye – not so good," he says. He shifts his body as if to get a little closer.

"You're right. Accident. Bad accident." His eyes are still focused on my patch.

"Bad, very bad." He repeats my word. He understands what I'm telling him. Good.

"Ahmik, my Pa goes to your village to trade. He told me that the eagle is special to the clan, but I don't know why. Can you tell me about the eagle?

"You know – the giant bird – the eagle. "Eeeeee, eeeeeee."

Ahmik's eyes open wide. He flutters his eyelids. "You are eagle boy." I feel a chill travel down my back when I hear those words. I look around wanting to see if anyone is nearby. Good, no one heard him call me, 'eagle boy'.

"What does that mean?" I smile broadly. "What does 'eagle boy' mean?" He must have seen what happened on the playground. I decide to ask more questions.

"Did you see the eagle come to help me? Why did he do that?" He stares without answering. I feel sweat running down my temples.

Suddenly he says, "You are special. When eagle follows someone and helps him, it means he is special. You are friend of eagle and eagle is friend to you."

Wow, he thinks the eagle is my friend. He thinks the eagle followed me on purpose. I need time to think about what this means.

"Can we be friends?" I search his face for an answer.

"Friends . . . friends?" Ahmik nods. I smile. He pulls the corners of his mouth back – not quite a smile, but I think it's good. We sit together in the cool shade. I'm content we're not talking. It gives me time to think. I have a new friend. I somehow sense we're connected. How weird is that?

Oh, oh, here comes Marian. She's headed straight for us. I knew she couldn't stay away. She'd die if she didn't know what we're talking about. She waves. She disappears behind the tree. Then her voice is behind me.

"Hi, Peter. Can I sit with you?" By the time I turn around, she's already next to us. She peeks at us with those twinkling blue eyes. She's talking to me, but her eyes are on Ahmik. Without giving me time to answer, she folds her arms across her chest, "Can I? I haven't met your friend, Peter, and I want to know about your eye."

Marian says she wants to know about my eye, but she really wants to know about Ahmik.

"Of course, you can sit here," I say. The corners of my lips curl back around my ears. I look at Ahmik, who is looking over my head. Then he turns away. My new friend doesn't look comfortable. He isn't so sure about Marian and he's not sure what to do next. He starts to get up.

"You don't have to go. Sit down, Ahmik. Don't leave. This is my friend, Marian. Ahmik, Marian's my friend."

I pat the dirt, and he sits down. Marian sits next to me. Ahmik looks from me to Marian. Her dark hair shines in the one beam of sunlight sneaking through the leaves. Ahmik's eyes stay on me. Pointing first at me he says, "Friends" and I nod. Next, he looks at Marian, points at her and pauses. Nothing but silence, then "My friend?"

"Yes, yes," she coos. A smile creeps across her face. Her eyes twinkle. Ahmik watches me then the corners of his mouth twist up ever so slightly like he's trying to smile.

Marian leans toward me. "Peter, can you take off the patch so I can see your eye? Do you see any light? Can you see shadows?" All I hear is a line of questions. My usual answers are, "I don't know or I'm not sure" or I just shake my head and usually she stops asking, but today is different. I decide to answer her. Maybe it'll be good if Ahmik knows about my eye too.

"I can take the patch off, but I have to warn you, it's not pretty. It's banged up. It's healing okay. I can see a little light and a little dark. It's weird - can't see any details, so I can't carve." I slide the patch up onto my forehead. A gasp slips between Marian's lips and her hand almost covers her eyes. She peeks at me from behind her cupped hand that stifles her sounds.

"I'm sorry, Peter." She hesitates then adds, "It doesn't look so bad. Some day it'll be as good as new." I don't think that's really true, but it's good that Marian is so positive. What else can she say? I know she's sorry for me. *Everyone's* sorry – most of all me.

"Pe . . . Peter, I want you to know about our clan's healer."

I shrug. Ahmik's creased forehead brings his black eyes closer so they almost touch. What is he about to tell me?

"I want you to know about how sick in my clan are healed. We have special holy man – a healer - our Shaman."

"What do you mean, Ahmik?"

Again he says, "Special man in clan – healer." Why is he telling me about someone in his village? I'm not sure I understand. Before I realize it, Ahmik's finger almost touches my face, but it doesn't. He pulls his hand back. Suddenly I'm hot and tense.

"Special Indian called Shaman. He helps sick people. Maybe he can . . ."

I flinch. Does he think someone in his clan can heal my eye? That sounds impossible – ridiculous – my folks would never go for that.

Shaking my head I say, "No one can help me. Dr. Barrett told Pa I could be blind in that eye. I just have to learn to live with it." Just the thought makes my heart streak around inside my chest and my voice quiver. I'll do anything to keep from being blind. I have to find a way to see again. I frown at Ahmik and Marian, who look concerned and troubled. Why should Ahmik worry? We just met. It's difficult to see how this puzzle is coming together. My new friend is talking about someone in his village who helps sick people. He wouldn't be telling me this if he didn't think . . .

"What do you mean, Ahmik?" When I'm not willing to talk, Marian takes over. "Why should Peter go to your village? Will this special person help Peter? Can he do something about his eye? Please, Ahmik. Tell us." Marian talks at top speed running all the questions together.

Ahmik looks lost. The questions stop. Marian realizes Ahmik can't follow her rapid questions. I'm not about to join the conversation. My mind spins out of control.

"It'll have to wait. Now's not the time," Marian says as kind of an apology to Ahmik. When I look at her face, I see an expression that tells me she'll probably lose sleep over my problem. What I don't see is a whole lot of patience.

Clang.

Clang.

Clang.

The sound of that bell seems louder than normal. Maybe my senses are on alert today.

The play area's shouts and laughter become silent. It's time to be serious again.

Walking back to our classroom, I'm not sure what happened under the tree. It takes a couple of minutes before I can follow Miss Prim's handwriting lesson. My thoughts are like crazy fish swimming in circles trying to reach the surface and get a gulp of air. Maybe it's best if I don't think anymore today.

*　*　*

The walk home takes longer than usual. I'm disappointed that Patches isn't on the porch. I like it when he runs up and welcomes me home. I push the door. And there stands Dr. Barrett talking to Ma. I know exactly what he's here to do. It's always the same – I know it by heart. Poke around, moan and then say I still have to wear a patch. I want to hear something different.

"Good afternoon, Peter. How's that eye doing?" Doc Barrett looks up from the white basin where he's scrubbing his hands.

"It's still here, Doc. I want it to change, but everything stays the same."

"Sit on the bench by the window where I have good light." His cold hands touch my cheek. I feel the patch letting go of my eyelid. He gently pushes my eyelid up, then moves the skin under my eye down. Now he's going to make that sound. Yep, I'm right. He utters the same sound, "Hmmmmm" that I hear each time he comes. Ma dumps the basin and fills it with fresh warm water from the kettle. He slips a soft cloth out of his bag, soaks it in the water and tenderly wipes my eye. This must be how he touches a newborn baby. He's so gentle. He pulls the lid down a little then pulls the skin under my eye out. I don't like it. My eye aches with sharp pains when he touches it, but it's not as bad as it used to be. I smell the salve that he uses. Bet he uses this stuff on everything. The same words go along with the new patch.

"Looking better, Peter. You're doing a fine job. I'll see you in two weeks."

I can't stand it. I want him to tell me I'm finished wearing the patch. I want him to tell me I'm going to see – even if it's just a little. But he doesn't. My stomach sinks.

Maybe it'll be good to think more about what Ahmik said yesterday. Maybe there is a special person in the clan who could help me. Ahmik seems to think that I should go to his village. Can't imagine getting permission from Ma and Pa to go there. It'll be like climbing the highest mountain around here. I don't know enough about the healer or what he does. I have to talk to Ahmik again before I can bring up the subject. All I know is there's something about the eagle that's mysterious and important. Maybe understanding more about the eagle will help me know if I should go to the village.

* * *

I must admit, the only reason I'm at school today is to find out more from Ahmik about his clan, the special healer he talked about and whether or not he thinks there is something that would help my eye. Too late now. I'll have to wait until lunchtime. I'll talk to Ahmik and Marian. I want Marian to be part of my plan. She asks great questions and because she's so smart, she'll think of things that I wouldn't think of.

Last night would have been a good time to talk to Pa. I could have found out what he knows about the Abamela. There'll be plenty of time to do that. Right now I need to know if I could even meet this healer. Ahmik called him a Shaman, but there's also someone called the Sachem. I get them confused.

* * *

Why do we have to spend the whole morning on Arithmetic? Dividing numbers is easy, but we have to repeat the lesson because the younger kids didn't understand it. Yesterday, Ahmik said . . . Got to stop my mind from wandering back to yesterday.

Good, the bell. I'll wait for Marian and Ahmik outside.

As soon as Ahmik is next to me, I ask, "Did you understand what we talked about yesterday?" My eyebrows arch and my head tilts to one side. His eyes narrow, his lips begin to move, but words don't follow. Before we can go on, Marian runs up.

"Are we going to sit under the tree and continue our plan?" She's already nodding as she speaks so I guess her mind is made up, and I guess she thinks we have a plan.

Marian shakes her head, "I'm not sure about a lot that was said yesterday. All I know is that we need more information before you can get our parents to agree. A trip to the Indian village is not a small thing. One thing is sure, Peter. I'm certain you'll carve before you know it. I just know it. You'll use that special white wood," she whispers. "I had a dream about it last night."

When I hear Marian's words, I know she's definitely planning to go with me.

Just because Marian dreamed it doesn't mean it's going to happen. What if it doesn't?

We settle under the tree. There's so much I want to know.

"Ahmik, what does Abamela mean?

"Abamela means "people of the great bird". We are also called "people of the sky." We have lived on these lands for hundreds of years. Each clan is like a nation. We make our laws and live by them.

Marian asks, "Is your language called, Abamela?"

"Our language is the Abamela-Penobit language. Members of the Penobit clan and our clan speak it. But we pronounce differently. When we speak, it sounds like music."

"Ahmik, please teach me how to say something. Please. Please." Marian pleads with Ahmik. He lowers his head. Then he says, "Sa-kai, sa-kai." This is greeting, Marian and 'shonisholi' means thank you." Marian says the two words a couple of times out loud while I repeat them in my head.

"Abamela people have same roles like your families. Men work and hunt. Women cook, grow food and care for the children."

"What kind of houses do you live in?" Marian asks.

When Pa and I went to the village, he explained that the Abamela didn't live in teepees like other Indians.

"Your people live in wigwams made from birch bark, right, Ahmik?

"Yes, Peter. You know about my village."

This is interesting, but what I want more information about is that special person who helps the sick.

"Ahmik, can you tell us about the person who . . ."

"Oh, yes, Peter. He's the Shaman in our clan. He's the healer. He has special powers, but you must meet the Sachem first. He is our clan's leader – the chief. You can not see the Shaman without the Sachem's blessing."

Marian is squirming like a worm on a fishing hook. She is very anxious, but she's being quiet. That's different. Just when I think Ahmik is going to go on speaking, Marian jumps up.

"We have to do this, Peter. Ahmik, you have to help us. I know this is what will help Peter. I'm sure of it." Ahmik and I stare at her. I don't know what to say. Ahmik is as still as one of my carved figures sitting on the mantel above the fireplace. What is he thinking?

"Ahmik, are you saying the chief of the clan has to give me permission to see the Shaman? Is that right?"

"You understand, friend Peter." My eyebrows curve upward, and my head pitches to one side. The space between his upper and lower eyelids shrinks while Marian waits to see what happens next.

* * *

"Peter, let's walk home the long way along the bluff. Ahmik can walk with us part of the way."

"Good idea Marian. We can stop at Pa's store and pick up the flour Ma asked me to bring home." As I smile, Marian giggles.

"Ahmik, you can come with us part of the way before you have to turn off to get to the village." This is good. I have my best friend on one side and . . . a new friend on the other.

Marian smiles at Ahmik. "I'm happy you can walk with us."

Today, Ahmik's lips form a real smile. He quickly shifts from Marian to me and his smile fades. Yep, this is good.

The wheat that Pa planted waves at us on the right and the dark ocean rolls in and out on the left. White foam rides on top of each wave until it crashes and disappears. It's a perfect autumn day. Marian stops and looks up.

"Listen," she says. "Where is it?" She tilts her head as far back as she can. Her hair touches her waist. We shade our eyes with our hands.

Nothing at first and then it's there circling – the eagle. Ahmik follows the eagle's screech.

"That's your eagle, Peter. The one that saved you," Marian shouts. She waves wildly. I gawk at it. Tears find my eyes. I don't understand why there are tears. Am I happy, or scared, or . . . I blink to force them back.

I need you. I need you. The phrase goes around and around in my head just like the eagle circling above us.

"Eeeeeeeee. Eeeeeeeee," its call pierces the air as it loops over our heads. The massive bird hypnotizes us as he dances before our eyes. I look at Ahmik. He runs in a circle tracing the path of the over-sized bird. I follow him, then, Marian begins her circles. Ahmik stops suddenly. I crash into him, and Marian can't stop in time. We collide. We laugh. Now Ahmik's eyes are closed, and he begins to chant. The syllables sound like a drum knocking inside my chest.

"Hep-a Hep-a Nay Nay, Hep-a Hep-a Nay Nay, Hep-a Nay Yan-na Hen-Nay Yo Way," he sings as the bird calls with his mighty cry.

Ahmik speaks first, "Peter, it's a sign. Eagle is the great symbol of the Abamela. It holds the power of my clan." He points a straight index finger at me then holds up two fingers. "Eagle came to you two times. Sacred sign. He is your eagle. The eagle only chooses special people. You are special."

Marian's mouth dangles open. I'm sure *she* wants to be special, but it can't be right now.

I feel strange as if a different energy – some secret eagle energy moves inside me. I want to follow the eagle. I don't know what it's all about, but I know I must find a way to go.

Marian studies me and her head moves up and down. I must know more before I can go.

"Ahmik, help me understand." My right foot kicks up a puff of dirt showing my impatience.

"We will know in the future, Peter. Much will be clear." There is something that makes me trust Ahmik. I know what he says is true. He doesn't have any reason to make it up.

Marian moves from one side of me to the other. I know she has something to say, "Peter, don't you think you should say something to your folks. You can't wait and then expect them to say 'yes.' She's right. I have to prepare them. But, I'm not sure what to tell them. They know medical doctors like Dr. Barrett and Indian healing is foreign to them. For that matter, I don't either.

The wheels in my brain slam to a halt. I really know nothing about what the healer does. I ask Ahmik, "Is it a ceremony? Is it dangerous? Is it painful? Will I be by myself?" I take a giant breath in order to continue. "Can my Pa be with me, or Marian, or you?" I don't give Ahmik time to answer although answers will help me make up my mind. I ask, "Do I have to stay in the village?" I've got to get answers. My Indian friend hasn't said a word. His eyes are deep and riveted on me. His breath is steady. Al last his lips move, "You must come to the village" Ahmik's words jolt me. Now, he tugs at my arm.

"No, no, I'm going home. Later – your village" I struggle with my answer and I struggle to free my arm.

Suddenly, Marian shouts, "I know what we have to do. Ahmik's English is pretty good, but we have to make sure Ahmik can translate _everything_ for you. You have to be able to ask him a lot of questions, and he has to be able to understand and answer you. He has to be your translator. You can't go to the village unless you understand everything that's happening."

Ahmik stands silently. Wrinkles take over my forehead and Marian's tightly held together lips form a single straight line. Even though her lips are sealed, her face wears a grin that tells me she's planning. Something she's good at.

Marian plays with her curls as they dangle next to her ear. At the same time, she ponders Ahmik, "Maybe after school next week, we can work together on English. We'll ask Miss Prim to help us. " Looking very satisfied, she brushes her hair back and lifts her cin. That's something she does when she's in control.

"I don't know." I begin to disagree.

Marian loves being in charge. Now she squares her shoulders and insists, "Of course, she will, especially if we tell her why it's so important for Ahmik's English to improve. She really likes you, Peter. She'll want to help."

Once more I try to speak, "I'm not sure . . ." but Marian puts her finger to her lips.

"Shhh," she tells me. There's no way I can disagree.

* * *

I can't help but wonder whether Marian's plan will work. She certainly is determined. I guess I'll see what happens today. The afternoon in school passes very quickly. I'm distracted thinking about how to get my parents to agree to our plan, and every time I look at Ahmik, he's leaning forward snatching each word as it floats in the air after it leaves Miss Prim's tiny lips. He's as anxious for this to work as I am and certainly Marian.

"Make sure you study the map for a test tomorrow," announces Miss Prim. Marian's already on her feet when Miss Prim says we can leave. Standing as close to me as she can, she whispers, "I'll talk to her – you'll see, Peter, this will work."

Everyone's pushing to get through the doorway. We lag behind. Miss Prim begins cleaning the board. Marian walks quietly to the front of the room. Miss Prim jumps like a little frog when Marian is at her side.

"Oh, Marian, you surprised me. I didn't know you were there." She peers over her glasses at Ahmik and me waiting by the door. Poor Miss Prim, she doesn't have any idea what Marian's about to ask her. She'll be surprised. Hope Marian's right. Her fingers are locked behind her back.

"Miss Prim, may I talk to you?" Marian begins in a most courteous manner.

"Of course, Marian. You seem a little worried. Is everything alright at home?" Our teacher takes a step closer to Marian and bends toward her so she can look directly in Marian's eyes.

"Oh, yes, Miss Prim. This isn't about home, it's about . . . it's very serious. It's about . . . well . . . it's about Peter and Ahmik and me. We need your help." The words sound desperate. They sizzle in the dry cool air.

"This sounds serious, Marian. Let's sit down while you tell me how I can help." Miss Prim pulls her chair close to the first student desk and motions Marian to sit. She takes Marian's hands between hers.

Words pour out of Marian's mouth like a rushing stream. "I knew you would want to help us. Peter's doctor isn't helping him regain his sight. A giant soaring eagle appeared twice. An Indian healer – a Shaman is an important part of Ahmik's clan. Marian stops to take a gulp of air so she can go on. Ahmik and I hold our breath. My body begins rocking. My palms are damp. We can't hear everything, but whatever Marian is telling Miss Prim seems to be working. I watch Miss Prim. She leans in, not wanting to miss a single word. She doesn't speak. Finally, she straightens up, shifts in her chair, then nods and motions for Ahmik and me to come forward. No words, just stares. She studies each of us. Her concentrated looks soft and her lips part in a loving smile. Words form on her lips. I'll faint if I don't get air, but I hold my breath. Miss Prim's index finger touches the tip of her nose and we wait for her thoughts. Why is it taking so long?

Finally, with one giant breath, she says, "I think it's . . . wonderful. I can work with all of you to help Ahmik become the translator. I will definitely help you." Marian takes a quick breath. A huge smile moves from her lips to her cheeks to her beautiful blue eyes until her whole face beams out and covers everything in the room.

"I knew it. I knew it," she sings. She's on her feet whirling around and around. I blink. Ahmik . . . well, Ahmik knows we're both happy. I look at his serious expression as it melts into a wide grin.

CHAPTER SEVEN

his is torture. Who cares about history? I want school to be over today so we can work on Ahmik's English. I'm not sure how we're going to do this, but Miss Prim has a plan. Miriam is fidgeting and squirming. It's like she's sitting on an ant hill. That's not like her. I wonder if Ahmik's face is tense. His face is scrunched up. His eyes are tiny slits. I asked him once why he did that with his eyes. He told me it helps him understand more. Maybe that would work for me.

There's the bell. Great. We had only a couple of hours left, but it seemed like a whole extra day. Now we can get to work.

Everyone's gone. Now it's just the three of us, and Miss Prim. Looks like she wants the chairs in a circle. She pushes one chair from behind her desk to the aisle in front of the student desks.

"Can I help you, Miss Prim?" I rush to her side.

"I'm fine Peter, thank you for offering. Let's all sit down. We're all going to have a part in Ahmik's English lessons. I know my plan will work."

Marian turns in the direction of every sound. Bet she doesn't want to miss anything. Ahmik doesn't blink. His eyes move from me to Marian without closing. My mind is ready, and my body has too much energy. Guess that's why my knees jitter.

"What should we do, Miss Prim?" Marian is her usual impatient self. She never wants to waste time.

"We'll begin in a minute. I have to explain a few things, we're going to use games, slate-boards, and a fun activity." I hear half the words. I look at Marian, who's crossed her arms so her hands hold tight to her shoulders. Her chin is tucked down. She arches one eyebrow. We have to get this right.

Miss Prim's vocabulary game is rapid fire. Words and meanings. She rings her brass bell and Marian, and I shout out hundreds of words, at least it seems like that many, and Ahmik shouts the meaning. Then, we have to use the word in a sentence. Marian doesn't have any trouble. I stumble. I don't understand why. I know these words. When Miss Prim holds up the card, I have trouble seeing it clearly. This patch gets in the way. If it's not that, it's nerves. Got to calm down. This is fun – challenging and fun, so why am I so nervous? Ahmik sometimes does better than I do. He's usually so quiet. I didn't realize how smart he is. I wish learning were like this every day.

* * *

It's the last school day of word drills. It's been three weeks and we all worked hard.

Miss Prim announces, "You are great with all the vocabulary words. Now we're going to act out difficult situations." She bustles about moving papers on her desk. She must be looking for something. "Ah, here's what I'm looking for." She rejoins the circle looking satisfied and ready to move on.

"All right. You're going to like this next practice. Marian, you're going to pretend to be the clan's leader. Peter, you'll be your father and Ahmik, well, Ahmik, you'll be yourself." Ahmik focuses on each of us. Miss Prim gives us pieces of paper with words that the character needs to say. Ahmik listens carefully to what we say. He translates without hesitation.

This is going to work. My mind races to thoughts of going to the village. Scene after scene, Ahmik understands and translates what the characters say.

When the scenes are finished, Miss Prim stands up, grins at us and says, "You're ready, Ahmik, to be Peter's translator. Your father will be proud of your English. You'll help Peter and the traders." I look at Ahmik. His usual straight, closed lips curl into his version of a smile.

"It's all up to us, isn't it, Miss Prim?" Marian asks. I'm glued to my chair. Marian, on her feet, turns like a spinning top. Suddenly, she stops squarely before our teacher.

"Yes, it is. My job is finished." Our kind teacher showers us with warm smiles.

"Thank you, Miss Prim," she says and reaches around Miss Prim's waist and gives her a hug. "Peter's trip to the Indian village will be much easier because you helped us." Marian's eyes flood with tears – I think they must be what Ma calls, happy tears. Ahmik is ready, and I, well, I was ready weeks ago.

"I'm very proud of all of you." Our teacher stands straight, shoulders back, head held high. She looks proud of us.

I don't think I've ever seen Miss Prim so happy. My eyes focus on Ahmik's grin.

I look at Ahmik squarely. "It's time for you to meet my mother and explain the healer to her." Ahmik jumps back, loses his grin and gains the look of an owl. I want to ask him why he's so surprised, but Marian's mouth is moving.

"Has your mother ever been to the Indian village? What do you think we should tell her and what about your father?" Before I can answer, she adds, "Maybe if your Ma is okay with your going . . . she'll help convince my father. It won't be easy. They never let me go anywhere alone."

"You won't be going alone, Marian, you'll be going with me." My stomach tumbles in every direction. "It's not going to be easy getting Pa's permission either." I close my eyes and picture how my father looks when his answer is, no. It's kind of a scary look. Don't like it.

"Marian, I think it's great you want to go with me. It'll be good having you there." She grins broadly.

* * *

The walk home is blanketed with stillness. My thinking is jumbled. Can't imagine what Ahmik is thinking and if I know Marian, her brain is planning the trip, step by step. Through the trees, I see Ma outside. She's taking the dry clothes inside. I run. Ahmik and Marian don't. By the time they catch up to us, I've caught my breath.

"Ma, I'd like you to meet Ahmik, my new friend from the Abamela clan. And of course, you remember Marian." Ma always liked Marian because she's so smart. Any time I said I wanted to study with Marian, Ma thought it was a good idea.

Patches gallops toward me. I bend down and stretch out my hand. He rubs his head under my hand. That's his way to telling me what he needs. His tag wagging is a sure sign he's happy.

Ma's smile is a winner. I see Ahmik's body relax. His shoulders slope down. They're not up to his ears. I'm certain Ahmik feels welcome.

"It's getting cool. Let's go inside. Maybe all of you would like a hot drink. Ahmik, have you ever tasted hot cocoa?" Ahmik's eyes go from my mother to Marian, then to me.

"No, Ma'am," he answers quietly.

"It's good, Ahmik. Just try it. I think you'll like it." Ma's voice is gentle and soothing. She peeks at Ahmik out of the corner of her eye. I like how Ma is trying to make him feel comfortable. We all go into the warm cabin. Only Patches stays on the porch waiting for Pa.

Ahmik lifts the cup and samples the warm chocolate tasting milk. I don't think he's ever had anything like this. I watch as he swishes some of the warm liquid inside his mouth.

"Um, good. Good. It's like honey – not quite as sweet, and not sticky either." His sips get bigger until the bottom of his cup is looking at the ceiling. Now he has a giagantic milk mustache. Marian laughs. Ahmik looks surprised not knowing why she's laughing.

"You have a milk mustache, Ahmik. You must think it's pretty good." Marian's words flit around the warm room as she settles into a place at the table. Ahmik senses he has something on his face so he wipes his mouth with his shirt sleeve, and a grin replaces the traces of milk on his face.

"Ma, where's my big slate-board?"

"In the corner by the front door, Peter." Ma looks up from where she's peeling potatoes, and the look tells me she's wondering what's going on.

When I bring it back to the table, Marian says, "Let's draw a picture of the Abamela village. Ahmik can tell us where to put the rows of corn and all the wigwams." It'll look like the actual village.

Ma comes up next to us looking at the slate-board.

"Is this your village, Ahmik?"

"Yes, Ma'am, my clan is the Abamela clan, and our village looks like this. It's not far from town. I walk to school every day."

Marian volunteers some information before I can make a sound.

"Ahmik invited us to go to his village, and he wants Peter to be healed by the clan's Shaman."

My jaw drops open. The heart that pumps blood around my body now sounds like thunder. I don't understand why Marian has to blurt out information that I want to tell. It's my story. It's my plan. Not hers. I was still thinking about what I wanted Ma to know . . . now, thanks to Marian, she knows everything. I paint an unsatisfied glare on my face so Marian will get my message, but she turns and smiles at my mother. I can't believe it. Now what? Ahmik stands like a silent white pine. He looks afraid. I bet he's uncomfortable that I'm so unhappy with Marian.

Somewhere in the background, my mother is asking, "Well, I see. I . . . well . . . I think we have a lot to talk about. Peter . . . do you want to tell me anything?" My head jerks and I realize Ma asked me a question. She has the unfinished drawing in her hands. Wrinkle channels form on her forehead – they always appear when she's waiting for an answer.

"Well?" Ma waits just long enough to see me shifting from my left foot to the right. "Are you going to tell me the whole story?"

A raging river of words lets loose and I can't stop them. All kind of feelings get mixed up with the words. They gush out of my mouth.

"An eagle," I begin. Without warning Ahmik, makes the sound of the giant bird, "Eeeeeee, Eeeeeeee. The eagle comes and saves Peter. Special. Peter is special," he says.

My turn. "Ahmik says the healer, the Shaman, in the village can help me – maybe even bring back my eyesight. I didn't want to go until we were sure Ahmik could be my translator. That's why we've stayed after school with Miss Prim. She helped us and now Ahmik is ready to tell me everything the Shaman says."

My mother stares. I stare. I can't tell how she feels or what she understands. I'm in the dark.

"Oh Peter, you've had frightening experiences: almost drowning, losing your sight in that eye, not being able to carve, being attacked by bullies. Oh my! But, everyone wants to help you, even Miss Prim. You should ask your Pa about going with Ahmik to the village. Maybe . . . maybe the Shaman can do what Dr. Barrett hasn't been able to do." I look into Ma's eyes and see the same desire that I have in my heart. She wants what I want.

Ma moves around the table. When she's deep thought, she hunches over, takes tiny quick steps, and you can see her searching her brain for answers. I've seen her do this before. When I look around, Marian is staring at me. I jerk my head toward the door. Marian and Ahmik follow me. The door bangs behind us.

"Sorry, Ma, for banging the door," I holler over my shoulder.

"Sorry Mrs. Poppin," Marian adds. Ahmik says, "Me too." I chuckle.

Outside, we yelp and squeal. We hold on to each other's hands so tightly I can't feel my fingers. Ahmik leads us tracing circles and loops around the garden. It's like we're imitating the flight of the eagle. Marian takes over and leads us in bigger circles.

"We're on our way," yells Marian. We fall to the ground and let go.

"Peter, I was wondering. Were you unhappy about something before?" Her voice is as sweet as a peach. I pause just long enough to know that I have to tell her.

"I was angry with you, Marian." My eyes search the clouds avoiding her eyes.

"Why? You were taking too long to tell your Ma about wanting to go to the village and it had to be said, so ... I did it," she states emphatically. "I only did what has to be done." Ahmik laughs out loud.

Ahmik and Marian are on their feet running down the road. Ahmik has farther to go to the village, but he's fast. Marian's cabin is closer. They'll both be home about the same time.

The ground pulls my energy into itself. I am still. My eye searches for the eagle in the darkening sky. I told Ma about the eagle saving me, but maybe she doesn't have to know everything. My head is suddenly filled with the screech of the eagle. My eagle. He was a speck in the sky.

Higher and higher he soared – his size shrank until he was gone. He was on his way to the heavens.

*   *   *

Pa's stomping the dust off his boots makes Ma jump. The door swings open, and the wind pushes him into the toasty room. He gives Ma a peck on the cheek.

"It was a long day, Mary. A couple of strangers came by the store. They bought some supplies – didn't say much. Had an odd way of talking. They sounded like they might have worked on ships. Looked like old weather-beaten sailors. They said they were new in town, and they needed work

"Mary, do we have any work around the cabin I could have them do?"

"Let me think on it, Tom"

"I'll find out what they're doing in town. Someone will know who they are," Pa adds.

"Did you go to the fields today, Pa?" I ask. With no rain, Ma worries about losing the crop. Everyone worries. Pa rubs his temples. His stressed look slowly fades.

"Everything is parched. We stand to lose it all if the rains don't come."

"Pa, I have an idea. All the townspeople could take empty barrels to the river, fill them and bring back the water. If we did it ten times, maybe it would be enough to save some of the crops."

"You're really thinking, Peter. That's a good idea, but we have too many acres of wheat and corn, but I'll tell the other farmers when we meet on Sunday. Thanks for the idea."

"You're right, Pa. It's not enough, but maybe we can think of something else." My Pa grins at me and as he walks behind me pats my shoulder.

"Tom. I know you're tired now, but Peter wants to talk to you about something important." I jump up and step toward my father. He puts down the cup of broth he was sipping.

"Sounds serious. What is it? Is everything all right at school?" My father now wears a concerned look on his weary face.

"Good, Pa, everything's good."

"Well then, what is it?" I'm fidgeting. My father notices. He asks again, "What is it, Peter?"

Words spill from my lips like water from a bucket. They won't stop.

"Pa, I don't think Dr. Barrett is helping me. I know it takes time, but . . . it's been several months, and nothing has changed. My friend, Ahmik, asked me to go to his village to see the . . . healer. . . it's a good idea to try something different." I need more air to go on, but I don't get the chance.

"Yes, yes, I know the village. That's where I trade." I forgot about Pa trading there. Maybe this will be easier than I expect. At least he knows where I want to go.

"Ahmik wants Peter to see their healer, a Shaman. He believes . . ."

I don't have a chance to finish. Pa's on his feet, shaking his head, moving around the room with giant steps. I don't want to hear him say, no, but I listen.

"I don't think that's a good idea, Peter. We know nothing about what they do. Let the village people use their healer and we use our doctor. Not a good idea at all. It's just going to take time, Dr. Barrett says. We have to be patient." My heart beats faster and faster as I realize how firm Pa is.

"Ahmik believes I'm special because the eagle comes to me." I can't quit. My voice begins to tremble, but I go on.

"The eagle is the symbol of his tribe and it is very unusual for the eagle to come to someone who is not a member of the clan. But he did, Pa. Ahmik tells me it's a sign." Pa makes a sour face wrinkling his nose. I stop talking long enough to sip at the air. My words float in the space around Pa.

Pa paces around the table, hands squeezed into his pants pockets, chin on his chest. His breathing has a rhythm. With two steps, his shoulders go up, and his chest goes out, then with the next two steps, he lets out a forceful exhale. Finally, the circling stops, and he comes to a halt in front of me. He takes his hands out of his pockets and puts them on my shoulders.

"Peter, I know you'd like to go to Ahmik's village and I'm certain you'd like to see with that eye, but I'm not comfortable with the idea of the Shaman. You don't know what might happen. Right now my answer is, no. We need more time." My body is stiff. I feel sick like I'm going to throw up.

"I'm sorry, Peter, but that's my decision. Do you understand?"

"Yes, Pa," I croak weakly.

My father studies me, turns and goes out to the porch. I wait. I glance at my mother. She doesn't look at me. She shows no expression, no way to read her mind – puckered lips and closed eyes. Then she quietly says, "Well . . . I have to . . . think, Peter." There's nothing to think about, is there?

It's been many months, and nothing has changed. What harm could come? I want to take the chance no matter the risk. I wish Pa knew that. I must go to the healer. I must. Got to start working on a plan. I wonder if Marian's folks said yes. Doesn't matter. I'm going, and that's that. Ma touches the top of my head as she walks behind me. I flinch. I look up as Ma gives me a fake smile. I nod.

"Who knows, Peter? Maybe he'll change his mind."

CHAPTER EIGHT

Outside, the birds squawk and twitter . . . I'm awake. One dream filled every inch of my mind and body last night. Even now, if I close my eyes, I hear the eagle, 'Eeeeee, Eeeeeeeee.' The eagle wasn't in my dream, but its voice was there – so clear. I remember the sound moving inside me, and I remember following the sound. I kept waking up and going back to sleep. I must have woken up a hundred times. Each time I went back to sleep, I had the same dream. I know it's a sign.

* * *

The kitchen isn't warm yet. Brrrrr. Ma just started the fire in the stove. It'll take a while to warm up the cabin.

"I didn't hear you, Peter. What are you doing up so early?"

"All night I dreamed about the eagle, Ma." My heart flutters.

"Pa doesn't want me to go. Ma, can you convince . . ."

Pa's feet shuffle along the floor as if he's too tired to lift them. He moves with a snail's speed coming to rest on the bench. He props up his head with his hands – elbows on the table.

"Are you feeling okay, Tom?" Ma asks in a barely audible voice.

"Just tired – didn't sleep well." He sips steaming coffee without looking up. My eyelids fall over my eyes. I can't look at my father. Finally, I peek out with my good eye, and I realize Pa's stare is fixed on me.

"How are you feeling this morning, Peter?"

"I'm okay, Pa." It's not really true, but I can't tell him what I'm really feeling. This is terrible. I've never lied to my folks, but I must go. Ahmik will help me, and he knows who I have to talk to. Now I have to talk to Marian. I do hope she can go.

* * *

Suddenly, Patches barks then howls. My father jumps from the table and runs outside to see what the commotion is. Ma follows. I can hear it - the sound - the distinctive screech of my eagle.

"Eeeeeeeee. Eeeeeeeeee." I run outside.

Ma stares and Pa's jaw falls open.

"I don't believe it. What is it doing?" Pa's shocked. He runs to the fence to get a better look. My grand eagle circles around our little cabin calling to me - maybe it's calling to my Pa. It cries over and over, *Go to the village . . . to the village . . . the village.* Of course, I'm the only one who hears its message, but that's okay. Maybe now, Pa understands.

* * *

I run all the way to school. My eye doesn't hurt like before, but it still doesn't let me see. I spot Marian.

"Marian, Marian, we've got to talk," I scream.

Marian runs toward me. "What is it, Peter? Did your Pa say, yes?"

"He said, no, Marian, no, but I've made up my mind – I'm going," I shout even though I'm almost on top of her.

"Stop shouting, Peter. Here comes Ahmik." Marian tugs at my sleeve.

"Ahmik, Peter's father won't give him permission to go to your village."

"What will you do?" quizzes Ahmik. I stare at my friends.

"Marian, did your parents say you could go?"

"They said, no, too, Peter, but . . .

"The eagle came this morning and circled around the cabin. Pa couldn't believe his eyes."

Without warning, Marian grabs my arm. "Maybe he'll change his mind."

"I don't have Pa's blessing, but I can't wait, Marian. I'm going.

Marian's cheeks turn pink. Her curls bounce around her face.

"And . . . what about you, Marian?" I ask my friend.

"I . . . oh, Peter, I . . ." Ahmik touches her arm and asks, "Well?"

"I'll help you with a plan, Peter, and . . . I'll go with you." I'm shocked at her words but happy that I won't be going alone. My mind shifts to the Sachem, Ahmik saying I might see, and the eagle . . . my eagle . . . that will guide me.

"Listen, we can talk about how to do this at lunch, ok?" My stomach is like the strings on the Parson's fiddle. Tight. My hands are sweaty, and I hear the nervousness that causes my words to wobble.

"Peter, I'm already putting together a plan. Ahmik will be a big help when we get to the village." Marian's face is serious, and Ahmik is his usual silent self. Suddenly, as we're about to enter the building, he says, "I know what I must do to prepare my village."

* * *

I'm relieved it's cool in the shade. The sweat has been rolling down my temples all morning, just thinking about what we're about to do.

"Peter, how long will it take us to walk to the village?" Marian doesn't walk as fast as I do and Ahmik walks even faster, but he'll be in the village waiting for us.

"Ahmik, how long does it take you to get home?"

"About twenty minutes, Peter."

"That means it'll take Marian and me about – double that."

"I'm not that slow, Peter." She shakes her head, and the curls go up and down like a spring. I didn't mean to hurt her feelings.

"It's good to have a little extra time so we can rest if we want to. We'll probably get there early, and Ahmik can show us around. How does that sound, Marian?"

"All right." She pulls her mouth back on one side, and I hear a little air escape from her nose. It's like when a gnat flies up your nose, and you want to get it out of there.

"What should I tell my mother? Should we take something to eat? How long will we stay there? You know I have to get home before dusk."

Questions flood our ears as Marian finds them inside her. She needs answers. I guess we all need answers.

"How about Sunday morning, early? We'll take fruit, some of Ma's cornbread if there's any left and . . . a sweater – might be cold when we come back." Ahmik's eyes are on me, but they shift to Marian and then back to me again.

"You can taste our food. We won't let you be hungry." He laughs out loud. This is the first time Ahmik has really laughed. I wonder what is so funny, but I don't ask.

"I'll tell Ma I'm going to your house, Marian, to help with your number work and Marian, you tell your folks we'll be working on building a model of our town for the coming fair."

"That sounds good, Peter." Ahmik grins and Marian's chin goes up and down, up and down.

"We're all set. Sunday morning at seven?" I watch my friends for agreement. The bell rings. "We did it. We have our plan. It's good – all good."

CHAPTER NINE

It's Sunday morning, and the sun's rays come through the slit between the curtains and I'm out of the cozy covers. I hope Marian is getting ready 'cause I don't want to go alone. The Abamela village is on the other side of town. I pack two apples, a chunk of corn bread and a sweater. I told Ma last night I was going to Marian's this morning. I'm sure she told Pa. Hope I can slip out before they start asking a lot of questions.

* * *

The road is so dusty. No rain. I walk faster than usual. Nerves I guess. Few people are out and about, but I see Marian. Can't believe she's ready and waiting.

"I'm so nervous, Peter. Are you sure we should go?"

"I've got to go, Marian. I want my sight back. If you don't want to go, it's okay. I understand."

"No, no, Peter, I'm coming with you. It's just that I'm nervous."

"Okay then, Let's go." I can tell Marian is really worried. Is she stressed because she lied to her parents or is she worried because she doesn't know what's going to happen in the healing? I suppose I'm uncomfortable about that too. I just have to risk it.

"Marian, see that man sitting on the steps in front of the jail? He's one of the strangers who watched me from the bluff. What's he doing there?"

"He looks strange in that hat." Marian's expression becomes colored with worry.

"Marian, I want to talk about the Shaman's healing, but I know so little about it. The only thing I know is that the Shaman uses his spirit animal, the eagle, to do the healing. Wish I knew more."

"Peter, I'm sure you'll learn about it when we get to the village." Marian looks down at her dust-covered shoes and stamps her feet. I laugh.

"They're only going to get dusty again," I say. She frowns.

As we get closer to the village, corn grows together with squash and tomatoes. The corn stands tall like warriors guarding the village.

"See those wigwams – Ahmik explains the one on the left is made of heavier hides, and it's good for winter. The other one doesn't have multiple layers of skins on it. It's covered with birch bark. It's for summer, much cooler." Women walk past us carrying babies on their backs and children run around with shabby longhaired dogs.

"Marian, I'd like to stay in the village for a while and learn their ways." She stares at me.

My mind skips to the Sachem, the great chief. I wonder what he's like. Ahmik told me I have to get permission from Bashaba, the Sachem before I can see the Shaman. His name is Messekiakkiak, the healer."

"I hope, Peter, we find out what their names mean in English. I like saying Messekiakkiak – it sounds like a drum."

The spirit animal of the Abamela clan and the great Shaman's personal spirit guide are the same – it's the eagle. Now I understand why the chief agreed to see me. There's a connection.

"Marian, there's Ahmik. He came out of that wigwam. Maybe that's where he lives. I wonder if he'll show us inside?"

"Hi, Ahmik. It didn't take us long to get here. It was a nice walk. There're a lot more trees on this side of town."

"I'm glad your trip was good, friend. I'm happy to see both of you." Ahmik seems different here in his village. He stands taller, and his voice is stronger. He's home here. I understand that.

Marian smiles at Ahmik and says, "I'm so happy you're helping Peter." Ahmik pulls his chin down to his chest and closes his eyes. A tall, strong looking man, walks in our direction. Ahmik spots him, waves and smiles broadly.

Ahmik's voice is clear and proud, "Peter, Marian, I want you to meet my father, Standing Bear." I know that name, but don't remember why. Ahmik looks like his father. Standing Bear's face sports a closed-lipped grin, and his eyes shine.

"It's nice to meet you, Mr. Standing Bear," I say. Marian smiles and does a little curtsy.

"Welcome, Peter. I know much about you from your father and from Ahmik." My Pa?

"How do you know my Pa?"

"Your Pa is Trader Tom. He comes to our village to trade copper pots for our furs. We make good business." Now I'm the one who grins.

"Ahmik has told me the reason you have come to see Bashaba. Ahmik told your story to everyone in the clan. The members voted to see if it was good for the son of the trader to see the great healer." Standing Bear stops and watches me. He looks like he's reading my mind.

"I have to ask, Standing Bear. Did they give me permission to see the Sachem?"

"Yes, Peter, the clan gave you permission. The eagle came twice to you. That was important in their decision."

"Actually, he came yesterday too, so it's really three times." I can't believe I said that. Standing Bear might think I'm too . . . Can't think of the word. Pa uses it when someone at a meeting keeps talking and interrupting without being asked to speak. Darn. Wish I could remember it. I'm sure it doesn't matter if the eagle came twice or three times. Just think, I have permission to see Bashaba.

I want to fly. I want to jump up and down. I want to howl, but all I can manage is a smile with my head moving up and down, first just a little and then in great fast brush strokes. My insides bubble with impatience. I have one mission – to see the healer.

Standing Bear examines me and after what seems like forever, he says very deliberately, "Now we'll see the Sachem. Bashaba will tell you of spirits and healing. You must understand our beliefs."

When I look over at Marian, she's as still as a rock. I'm not sure she's breathing.

"Can I come with you?" she whispers.

"Yes, yes, of course," I blurt out. Then I think it would be good to ask Standing Bear.

"Mr. Standing Bear, can Marian come with us?"

Standing Bear crouches down so he's eye to eye with Marian. "It will be good for him to know you're there, and you will understand what is going to happen."

We follow Standing Bear to the Sachem's wigwam. Bashaba appears outside the wigwam. Tall and straight, with a weathered, wrinkled face, he has the look of a warrior. His arms show scars and tattoos.

Bashaba motions to us, "Come . . . sit. I will tell you about spirit guides. You must understand how the spirit guide joins the Abamela to the Great Spirit. The mighty Bald Eagle connects our clan to the heavens. The eagle is special for keen sight and powerful flight. The beating of its giant wings brings rain from the sky. The eagle brings rain. Water washes and heals. We ask the eagle for rain first then healing. When the eagle soars over your head, it is a sign that healing rain will come. An eagle's eye is sharp, keen. Deep in your mind make a clear picture. Changes will come to your life. What needs healing, Peter?" The tall man whose eyes pierce me listens for my answer. It's difficult to find my voice. I dig deep inside.

"My eye needs to be healed," I answer.

"The Shaman uses his own spirit guide, mighty Eagle, to reach the Great Spirit for healing. Water will clean your eye, Peter. You prepare. Think good thoughts. Know the eagle is your guide. The eagle will bring lightning and thunder in a storm. The eagle will give you special vision." His words stop, then he says, "Now, it's time to meet Messekiakkiak. Do you understand, Peter? Do you understand, Peter's friend?"

"Yes, yes, I'm ready." My heart is wild inside me. My hands form tight fists. Everything inside me is dancing around. I turn to Marian whose face has lost its color.

"He's ready, Mr. Bashaba. I know he is." Marian can't hold back her words. She is as excited as I am. Not knowing anything about the healing worries me, but I'm not afraid. I'm ready . . . no matter what. I'm glad Marian is here.

"Ahmik, what do we do now?"

"I'll be there with you. Don't worry, Peter. We're going into the Shaman's wigwam for the healing. I will translate everything Messekiakkiak says." The look on my face says I'm afraid.

"Don't worry, Peter. Marian and I will be with you. We're here to help you." I take two deep breaths and try to let our all my nervous energy.

* * *

The Shaman's wigwam is much larger than the others – drawings in vivid colors stand side by side on the animal hides that cover the dwelling. Eagles soar, swoop, perch high atop trees. One's giant wingspan reaches out to the next wigwam. Standing Bear stands fast with us. Some native women come up behind us. They carry small skin drums. I can't find Ahmik. I want to call out to him, but somehow I know I have to wait. He'll be there to translate. I trust him.

The narrow oval opening to the Shaman's wigwam looks like an entrance to a tunnel – I'm not sure what's inside. Marian's hand is on my shoulder – not pushing, not moving, just being there. I feel confident. I stop thinking. I follow Standing Bear, and I see Ahmik, who gets in line next to his father. Marian follows me. A step forward, then another and another until I'm enveloped in darkness. I sense my friends' strength surrounding me.

An unexpected honeyed odor creeps into my nostrils. I feel my eyelids closing over my eyes, and I breathe deeply taking in the scent that cloaks me. It is the scent of the Great Spirit. I sense my blind eye hidden beneath its patch, my perfect-sighted eye opens and stretches to adjust to the dark feeling of the unknown. I want to tear the patch off, but I know it's not time. Shadows begin to pop in and out of my focus. I blink once, twice, again and again as if to clear a haze from my vision and then I'm there – I'm standing in front of the great healer, Messekiakkiak.

He sits perfectly still on a woven red and black blanket. Eyes closed. Is he real or is this but a carved statue. My eye finally focuses, the greatness of the healer becomes crystal-clear. He is more than what I had imagined. He wears an animal hide vest with a beaded soaring eagle hanging around his neck. His arms decorated with a pitch-black circular pattern that begins at his wrists and as the bands move up his arms, they grew wider. Between the bands are eagle tattoos. It's the circling eagle. Talons hang over his shoulders. They look like they are ready to lift Messekiakkiak into the heavens. A feathered braid drapes over his right shoulder. I lift my sight to the Shaman's face. The head of an eagle faces me. White paint creates the head and the feather-like painting travels down his neck and ends in black feathers. Yellow-orange paint covers his long beak-like nose until it touches his lips. It's the eagle's beak. Black circles his eyes. With a black dot on his lids, the eagle stares at me. Messekiakkiak opens his eyes and finds me. No one speaks, but I know I'm to take a seat cross-legged opposite him. It's as if I'm following a command. Standing Bear is next to me and Ahmik takes his place to the right of the healer. Marian is sitting in the circle of women. I don't know when she left her place behind me. The women move in a circle around us. Marian moves with the women. One begins to drum a soft, steady beat keeping time with my heart.

Messekiakkiak uses the Abamela-Penobit language. Ahmik translates.

"You are the eagle kin. You are 'one seeing eye'. You need healing," Ahmik states clearly what the Shaman says.

I know he hasn't asked me to answer him, but I can't help myself, "Yes, I had an accident. A piece of wood hit my eye and scratched it. I can't see. I want to see so I can help my father, and I want to carve . . . eagles."

I watch Ahmik as he leans into Messekiakkiak. In a whispered tone, he tells the Shaman what I said. The healer utters something to Ahmik. When he finishes, Ahmik turns to me. Concern forms deep creases on his face. He looks again at the healer whose eyes have disappeared behind his heavy painted eyelids. He waits until the drumming is softer, then speaks to me, in a deep voice. It doesn't sound like Ahmik. His voice is deep and far away, but I know it is my friend who is about to give me the healer's message.

"Peter, rain comes to wash your eye." A moment later, a clap of thunder sounds outside the wigwam and a couple of lightning strikes can be heard. The skins of the wigwam shudder.

"It can't be," I murmur, "Rain . . . rain is . . ." but my voice trickles away. In that moment, we - me, Marian, Ahmik, and Standing Bear are certain something unusual is happening. I don't think I understand, and I doubt Marian understands, but I remember Ahmik told us it was all good.

"The Shaman will soar to meet the Great Spirit and ask for your sight to return," says Ahmik. "Lie still, Peter, on this blanket. Don't move. Take off the patch. Close your eyes and see your eagle flying around your head." I follow his directions.

Faster and louder, the drumming fills the space. The women chant the same syllables over and over. With my eyes closed, I see my eagle circling closer and closer. Then, I see the healer extend his giant wings and soar into the black sky. My eagle hovers above me, and circles in slow motion.

"Peeeeter, Peeeeter." A voice calls me from the heavens. "You . . . have new sight . . . the eye of an eagle." My heart stops and then bursts. I am desperate to open my eyes, but I won't or maybe I can't. Am I afraid? No. No. I'm not afraid. I want to see. I don't care what I see. I just want to see.

The eye . . . of . . . of an eagle? How? What does that mean? The drumming is faster, and my heart matches its every beat. It's water I feel. Drop by drop, it's falling on my eyes. It's cool. How strange – it doesn't run down my cheek. It's disappearing into my eyes. My body wants to move, but it's stiff, like a board, but my heart - my heart is outside me, and it's still. Absolutely still. How can that be?

Time isn't moving. The world isn't turning. The sweet aroma and the rhythm of the drums make it all stop. All I can do is wait for some word, some sign, some message to wake up, but there is only silence, a stillness, a deafening quiet. Just wait. Wait.

"Yes, Messekiakkiak." Ahmik's voice sounds like it's under water. What is Messekiakkiak telling him? I'm as still as a lizard waiting for its dinner to fly by. Again, Ahmik speaks, "I will tell him, great Shaman."

"Peter, don't open your eyes. Messekiakkiak wants you to know what it means to have the eye . . . the eye of an eagle." The words, 'eye of an eagle' skip around and around in my head.

"Peter, listen carefully – it means that you will see again, but you will see the world differently. Sometimes . . ." Ahmik stops mid-sentence. His breathing is jittery.

"Sometimes you will see the past . . ." Ahmik stumbles with the words, inhales deeply and continues, "You will look into the past. Do you understand?"

I can't find my voice. What does it mean – to see the past? I don't – can't understand.

As if Messekiakkiak can read my thoughts, he says, "It is good, Peter, it is good."

"Good," I repeat. My mind spirals toward the sky seeing the past months. I can see it all. I see the cliff where I fell. I see the white driftwood that I'll be able to carve now for my mother. I see the dirty silver mystery object covered with torn blue cloth that I took from the beach. I see Miss Prim, Dr. Barrett and even the boys who teased me. Everything washes before my eyes.

"Marian's trembling voice murmurs, Are you okay, Peter?" Her voice jolts my eyes open, and it's all there. I see everything clearly with both eyes.

"I can . . . I can see! Ahmik, Marian, I can see. Both eyes see you." I look around. My voice doesn't sound like me. It is clear and definite.

Ahmik whispers, "Now you will see a different world. The healer says you must use the box."

"What? How?" Silence follows.

CHAPTER TEN

I don't remember how long the healing ceremony took, and I don't remember leaving the Shaman's tent. It seems like I had a dream, but I know it really happened. I stand taking in my surroundings. I shake my head to clear it. I know it's time to leave the village and go home. Marian just stares at me.

"Peter, are you all right?" she asks in a whisper.

"I'm good, Marian, but I have something I must do." What words do I have that could possibly thank Messekiakkiak, Bashaba, Standing Bear and Ahmik for all their help with my healing. 'Thank you' – two little words – seem too simple, but I can't think of anything else. I turn back toward the entrance to the Shaman's wigwam, and the three Indians are standing, their eyes peering into my heart. My heart beats faster.

"Thank you . . . thank you for my sight." My eyes find each of their faces and my heart reaches out to them.

"Go, Eagle Boy. Use new sight to do good work." Bashaba's voice is low. His words wrap around me. I'm warm inside.

"We have to go, Peter, it's late." Marian stands next to me. Her skin is the color of cream. Her cheeks are bright cherry pink. I feel her hand enclosing mine. She tugs just a little. "Let's go, Peter. Thank you, Mr. Standing Bear. It was a wonderful healing." Marian is talking probably because I'm not.

"Good bye friends," I form the words ever so thoughtfully.

"Good bye, Peter."

Each step is new like I'm learning to walk again. I'm not sure why. Marian is pulling me by my shirtsleeve.

"Okay, I'm coming. There's so much I want to talk to you about, but my words are stuck. They can't move off my tongue." What I notice is everything – like I've never seen any of it before. It's all so beautiful.

"Peter, I know you don't want to talk about what happened, but we've got to talk about what we're going to tell our parents." When I hear her words, I shiver. She's right. Panic begins to rumble inside me.

"Pa's going to be so angry. I'm sure to be punished. I think . . . we need to tell our folks the truth."

"Oh, my," Marian's lips quiver and her breathing quickens, "Oh, Peter. I'm scared." We get to the crossroads. We have to leave each other.

"It'll be okay, Marian. I know it'll be okay. Just tell them the truth." She walks away with tears in her eyes. I feel guilty. Being healed was worth it, but I feel bad that Marian is going to be in trouble. Not good.

*　*　*

I don't like getting home in the dark. Makes everything worse since Pa tells me always to get home before dark. Not much I can do about that now. It's cold, but my hands are sweating. If I can open this door without too much noise, I can . . . Patches lets out a small bark as the door swings open.

"Thanks, Patches," I mumble.

"Peter, is that you? Where have you been?" My feet don't move. They're stuck. All I can do is breathe in and out, in and out. Hot air from the fireplace brushes my cheeks.

"I know you heard me, mister. I asked you a question. You weren't at Marian's cabin. Where were you?" Pa's look is enough to stop a bear. His voice bellows like a bull moose.

"No, sir, I wasn't at her cabin, but I was with here. We . . ." I better just tell him the truth. "I had to go, Pa, I had to – I wanted to be healed. I wanted to see, Pa, and . . ." My thoughts run up against each other. Tears run down my cheeks. "I'm sorry, Pa. I had to go . . . I just (sob, sob) had to and Marian went with me."

The air is filled with tension. Patches can feel it. He goes to a corner so he's out of the way.

"Peter!" Pa's voice shakes me. "I don't know what to say." Ma hasn't moved a muscle. She doesn't say a word – not with Pa being so angry.

I take a chance. "Pa, I . . . I can see, Pa. I can see with both eyes." My voice is sickly. I don't know if Pa hears my words. He doesn't say anything. Should I say it again? I'd better not. I wait for something to happen. Nothing moves. Time stops.

"Go to bed, Peter. I'm too angry to talk about this now. We'll talk tomorrow." He's *really* angry. My feet inch along the floor. Tears hit the floor.

"I'm sorry. I'm so sorry, but . . . I can see with both eyes."

My heart splits in two. I bury my head in the quilt. My arm slides out of bed and comes to rest on Patches already asleep. Two deep breaths and . . .

* * *

What happened yesterday? Was I dreaming, or was it all real? I don't remember walking home. Was Marian with me? Did I tell my parents about the healing? I've got to talk to Marian. I'm not certain what day of the week it is. All I can do is stare at the ceiling. I cover my hurt eye. Look at all those imperfections in the wood. If I cover the first eye with my hand and peer again at the ceiling, I can see as much detail in the unfinished rough wood with my injured eye as I did with the good eye. They're both good now. I want to shout my discovery to my parents, but it's barely dawn. Why is this patch here? I must have put it on before I got home. Bashaba, the leader of the clan and Messekiakkiak, the healer pop into my mind. I see them clearly, but then everything is a blur. I must try harder to picture it in my mind. Something sweet, drumming, eagle tattoos . . . Ahmik . . . yes. I must be still. I want to remember what else happened.

"Peter, are you coming to breakfast?" Ma's calling me. "You'd better hurry. Don't want to be late for school." Guess it's Monday – a school day. This will be interesting. I wonder where Pa is. Am I going to get it before school? Well, what I get, I get.

"I'll be right there," I shout. I climb out of bed and notice my dog isn't there. The scenery is more than beautiful. The best part is I see it all clearly.

"Ma, Ma, I can see everything. It's all perfect," I call on my way to the table. I want to see Ahmik to thank him, and I've got to see my friend, Marian. Hope her parents let her be my friend.

"Ma, are you angry that Marian and I went to Ahmik's village?"

"Yes, Peter, I am. Pa and I were disappointed that you didn't tell us the truth. When you explained why you went, Pa said he understood that you just had to go, but he said you must never lie to us again."

"I'm very sorry, Ma. Pa had said, no, and I just . . . " I examine my hands, each knuckle, each fingernail. I can't look at my mother. I caused both of my folks a lot of pain – now they won't trust me. Tears spill out onto the table. "I'm . . ."

"We want to know everything, Peter. Yesterday you didn't tell us much. We don't know what happened. Pa sent you to bed."

"Ma, do you know I can see?"

"What do you mean, Peter – see?

"I can see everything clearly, Ma, like before the accident. It's a miracle."

"I'm not sure I understand, Peter. You'll have to tell us what happened at the village. I'm happy for you. Maybe now, life will be normal."

I think about the Shaman's words, "You'll see the past" and I know life is going to be anything but normal.

"Peter, you're going to be surprised when you see the shed. A man came by looking for work. Pa had to do some work in the shed, so he was there. He did a good job. Now you can start to work on your carving." My mind races. Is that the same man I saw on the cliff?

I don't think Ma will understand the sight of an eagle. I stop what I'm doing and listen, but all I hear are the usual morning birds. Guess I was hoping to get another eagle visit. All the details about the healing seem fuzzy. I have to recall as much as I can so I can tell Pa and Ma. Marian should be able to help. She has a great memory.

What does it mean to see the past? For now, I can't think about it, I have much carving to do. I have a mermaid to carve and ... there's still the secret object hidden in my winter coat pocket.

"Ma, where's my warm jacket? I want to wear it today. It's cool outside."

"It's on a peg in the shed, Peter." I disappear. Patches is right behind me. Once inside, I walk over to the pegs on the wall and finger the jacket.

"Here's the lump. It's still here, Patches."

I take it out and examine it. Kind of heavy, dirty and crusty. Still smells like the sea. My fingers close around it. What's that? A flash of light. I shake my head and close my eyes. Flashes of light and dark play behind my eyelids. What's going on? What's happening?

"Peeeeeter, what are you doing out there? You've got to get going. You'll be late," Ma's voice shakes me, and the light and dark images vanish. I feel sick. I don't understand what just happened. I'll put this back in my pocket. Think I'll finish my half-eaten breakfast. All I need is one more bite of bread.

"See you later, Ma."

"I'll be home after school, doggie." Another pat on his head and I'm out the door.

Everything looks so different. The shapes are so clear. The lines, the forms, and the bright colors are truly grand. Truly amazing. I don't remember my sight being this clear

* * *

Wow, what's going on? The schoolyard is buzzing with excitement. They must have heard my good news. I don't have my pirate patch.

"Peter, Peter, we heard you can see. Is it true?" A million voices and they all want to know the same thing. Even the bullies line up to see my eye.

"Yes, I can see."

Like in a singing group a long 'Ahhhhhhhhhhh' fills the air in unison. Now I've got a dilemma. Should I tell them about the Shaman and the healing in the wigwam? Maybe – maybe not. Ahmik appears out of nowhere. He whispers in my ear, "Don't tell them about Messekiakkiak and the healing." I stare at my friend and know he's right. I can't reveal the secrets of the clan. Ahmik warns me, "Our ceremonies are sacred, special – not to be shared with outsiders. You are special. Please . . ." I nod. He lets go of the tension. His face softens and his shoulders fall.

"How did it happen, Peter? Tell us," Jacob asks.

"It's rest and time," I explain. I see Marian. She listens, eyebrows to the ceiling, but saying nothing.

"Let's all go inside," I say trying to avoid more questions. Once inside, Miss Prim begins to ask something. She looks at Ahmik. The scared look on his face tells her a lot. She seals her lips.

"Peter, we're very happy you can see again. Welcome back. Children, let's give Peter our congratulations." Smiling faces. Hands clapping. This feels good. Everyone's happy for me.

* * *

Ahmik and I have no problem catching up with our lessons. Waiting for the lunch hour is agony. I'm on edge about talking to Marian. Finally, class is over, and we meet behind the school building.

"Marian, my mind is foggy. You have to tell me what took place in the Shaman's wigwam." Drop by drop, as if an expensive tonic, she recalls with vivid details of our adventure . . . I don't think she's forgotten anything. She doesn't speak of the outcome. She's not sure she should. I think about my Pa. I bet he would have sacrificed anything to see the Shaman, painted like an eagle, hear the drumming, and smell the strange fragrance. I've got to tell him the whole story.

Ahmik tells Marian to raise her right hand. "You can't breathe a word – not a single word . . . to anyone. Swear."

"I swear," she breathes.

"I won't tell anyone – I promise," she whispers crossing her heart with her index finger.

* * *

My studies are caught up. My folks know most of the details of the healing, and it's time to focus on carving Ma's mermaid. These fingers will coax the white driftwood into a graceful mermaid. I must take my time. This carving has to be perfect. The tail is beginning to look like what I have in the sketch. Every scale is perfectly proportioned and placed. It's taken two weeks, but I'm ready to carve her long wavy hair to look like a golden chain falling onto her shoulders. Ma's going to love her. The last thing I have to do is put this loop on her back so Ma can hang her anywhere. That won't take long. With both eyes to see with, it's easy to remember everything about carving. I think I'll give Ma her gift after dinner tomorrow.

*   *   *

"Peter, dinner's ready." Boy, I'm lucky. It got late very fast. It's just in time. I'll hide it until we finish the meal. Finally, dishes are off the table.

"Ma, can you come and sit down?" She dries her hands on her apron, looks at Pa as if he knows something about what is going on, but he raises his eyebrows in an 'I don't know' look. I hide my gift behind my back, "I made something for you. It took longer than I wanted, but I finished it, so Happy Birthday." My hand shoots out from behind my back. The mermaid comes face to face with my mother. She's stunned, shocked, amazed.

"Peter, this is the most beautiful birthday gift you've ever made me. It's a treasure – I'll hang her over the fireplace so we can all admire your work." Tears flood her eyes. She wipes them away with a corner of her apron. "It's just too wonderful." Pa looks pretty surprised too.

"She's absolutely perfect, Peter. What a fine piece of carving." He beams his approval. I'm satisfied.

With the mermaid finished, I now have time to examine the secret object.

"Ma, I'm going out to the shed. I have something to do out there." I light the oil lamp. It brings a warm glow to my little workshop. Won't take me long to get a little fire going. Then, I can examine it.

So . . . I pull the package out of its hiding place. I carefully place the crusty fist-sized object on the old scarred table. I eye the odd shape hiding behind its brittle covering. My fingers pick at it.

"Nothing's breaking off. I'll try this chisel. Good for chipping away the bark of an old tree, so it should be good for this too."

I lean into it. A piece of the hard material flies off like a shooting star and lands on the floor – then another. Patches jumps each time a piece hits the floor.

"You'd better get in the corner, boy." He trots away.

"Good boy. Would want any of this stuff to hit you." This tool is perfect. Shouldn't take too long.

The better part of an hour goes by. The fire crackles letting me know it's hungry again.

"What an appetite. Okay, okay – here's another piece of wood." I work until Ma's voice calls me into the cabin.

"Ma, can I invite Ahmik and Marian home tomorrow?"

"Good idea. I'll have fresh cornbread waiting." There is absolutely nothing as delicious as Ma's cornbread. Of course, her apple pie won a prize at the festival last year. But tomorrow it's cornbread.

"I hope they can come. Need to show them something. When's Pa coming home?" Just then, the cold air pushes the door and Pa with his black porcupine hair into the toasty room.

"Windy out there. Think a winter storm is on the way," mutters my out-of-breadth father. I watch as he bends down to give Ma a peck on the cheek. As he walks behind me, I get a slap on the back, and he asks, "Your day, Peter?"

"Great, Pa. Miss Prim talked about shipwrecks. She said they were pretty common along this coast. "Were there any around here, Pa?" Coming to the table after hanging up his plaid woolen jacket, Pa gives me an odd look.

"As a matter of fact, Peter, there were. A famous pirate ship sank . . . hmm . . . let me think . . . when was that?" Ma wrinkles her brow. Pa notices. Stopping mid-sentence, he looks up at Ma, "Right now – I'm starving – let's eat. We can talk about pirates later."

The aroma of garlic, onions and tomatoes stewing together talks to my grumbling stomach. No more questions.

CHAPTER ELEVEN

After dinner, Pa doesn't bring up the topic of pirates. I know I have something waiting in the shed, so I let it go. I'm more anxious to work on freeing whatever is under all the sea debris.

Chips fly off in every direction. I hope I'm not damaging what's under all this hard stuff. Interesting . . . the hardened cloth is stuck to some barnacles. I don't want to tear it. I remember how the doctor soaked my bandages. Maybe that will work. I want to save the blue cloth, but tiny bits of it are coming off. Can't help it. I've got to do this with patience. There it is – a round silver box with some kind of initials on it.

"Peter," Pa calls breaking the still night air, "You'd better come in. School tomorrow."

"Okay, Pa." I hate having to stop. I waited this long . . . guess one more day won't kill me.

* * *

After school, Ahmik, Marian and I walk slowly home. "Mom made cornbread today," I announce. With just the words, my mouth begins to water.

"Yum, warm milk and fresh baked cornbread will fill our hungry stomachs," Marian adds with a grin.

"Where's your dog, Peter?"

"He's probably with Pa in the field or at the store."

"He's really a wonderful dog. I wish my parents would let me have a dog." Marian's eyes reveal how sad she is not having a dog. As she watches me, I make an attempt to smile, but decide it's better if I say, "I understand. You can come over any time you want and be with Patches." The sadness fades in her blue eyes and she's back to being Marian.

"Let's go to the shed first. I have something to show you," I whisper.

"What is it?" Marian answers in an almost hidden voice.

"It's in the shed. Wait till you see." I push the door so hard, it bangs against the wall.

I lead them over to the object and point directly at it.

"Doesn't look like anything special," Marian says, lifting her left shoulder and looking over the edge of it.

I give her an annoyed side look without moving my head. I snap, "It's dirty and needs cleaning. You'll see. I had to chip away at the crust. This blue cloth had a strong hold on it. I wanted to save as much as I could, but it was impossible. Bits of the cloth came off with the crusty stuff. The box was under the cloth. It looks like it might have been some kind of pouch."

"Looks like it might be sil . . . ver," Marian stutters.

"Silver." I repeat the important word.

Ahmik, who has been quiet asks, "Have you tried to open it?"

"No, not yet, but I think there are some initials on the top. Can you read them, Marian?"

"Not exactly . . . looks like that fancy old English writing. We'll have to ask Miss Prim."

I'll be right back. Got to get something to clean this with. I know just the thing.

"Ma, where's your cleaning powder?" I search through Ma's storage chest.

"Whatever for, Peter?" Not waiting for me to answer she adds, "Should be in there. Don't waste it."

With the powder, the three of us take turns rubbing the object. In a short time, the light from the oil lamp twinkles on the raised letters. This really is a treasure. I remember how I saw flashes of light when I held it before. It only happened once. Got to remember exactly what I did so it will happen again. What was I doing? My friends look bewildered.

"I'm thinking. I'll tell you both what's going on as soon as I have it. I got it . . . I know . . . I know," I blurt out.

"What do you know?" Marian says with an air of not caring. I know she cares, but she's impatient.

"When I held the object, I closed my eyes and … light and dark flashed behind my eyelids." Arms fold in front of Marian's chest and pursed lips twist her mouth to one side.

"So?" That's what she says when she's tired of waiting.

"Watch, just watch." This better work or my friends will be out of here. Here goes.

The room and everything in it watch as I draw in the heated air. It's a forever breath. I exhale as if emptying a bucket. I inhale a second time. I hold on to the box carefully wrapping my fingers around it, look with saucer eyes at my friends then clamp my eyelids down tight. My upper and lower eyelashes are smashed together, wrinkles crease the corners of my eyes. My lips - a tight line. Nothing happens, then . . . light . . . a flash . . . a shape. What's that? It looks like . . . it can't be. It's a ship. Startled, my eyes jerk open. I jump back and drop the box on the table. Ahmik and Marian are speechless. Blank stares – no expression, no color.

Marian gasps, "Peter, what happened? Your eyeballs were twitching behind your eyelids. What did you see? Tell us what happened."

Ahmik finds his voice, "You saw something from the past, didn't you? It's beginning, Peter. Remember what the Shaman said?

Marian screams, "I have to know. What's going on? I'm your friend. We 're in this together." Marian's cheeks blush scarlet while water finds its way into her eyes. Each drop glistens against her black eyelashes. "I was there, but there are things I didn't hear. I want to know what the Shaman said. Is that what this is all about?"

"Okay, Marian, I'll tell you, but you *can't* absolutely *can't* tell anyone. The Shaman and his healing ceremony can't be known by outsiders . . . *you're* an outsider – even though you were there."

Ahmik's eyes are as dark as a moonless night sky. He inches in her direction. A few inches taller than Marian, he waits, and watches. "Remember, Marian, the Shaman flew to the heaven and asked the

Great Spirit to heal Peter. Peter was healed because he is special and the eagle is his protector." Marian's eyes clear, she stops sniffling. Not one syllable skips off her tongue. When Ahmik sees Marian relax, he continues, "Peter got his sight back, but it's not like he had before. It's . . . well, it's different."

Peter adds, "Tell her, Ahmik, or I will."

Ahmik hesitates. "Peter was given the eye of an eagle. He can see things in the past. That's what happened before."

Marian's eyelids beat like the wings of a hummingbird. "That's absolutely ridiculous. How could you see the past? I don't . . . I can't believe it."

Ahmik answers her doubt. "Marian, I know it's hard to believe, but it's true. Peter, tell her what you saw when you held the box."

I collapse into the chair, cradling my head in my hands. Marian is upset, but I can't help but wonder if she will tell the secrets of the tribe to everyone at school. Nausea finds its way into my mouth.

Marian touches my shoulder. "I'm sorry, Peter, for upsetting you. It's just so hard to believe, but I do believe you and Ahmik. I promise, cross my heart, I promise not to tell anyone. Do you trust me, Peter?"

"Of course, I do, Marian."

Hope I'm not making a mistake. I'm not sure why Marian is upset. She was there. She said she didn't hear everything. That may be true, but maybe she doesn't understand eye of an eagle.

*　　*　　*

Every day is exciting. After school, we meet at my cabin and immediately go to the shed. That's when I curl my fingers around the box, close out the world and wait for images of a time gone by to come to me.

"Ahmik, Marian, sit across from me and take each other's hands. I'm not sure what's going to happen, but I want the two of you to listen – listen to everything I say."

Marian's timid voice asks, "Peter, do you . . . do you think you can tell us what you're seeing?"

"I'm not sure. I'll try my best."

As I take the box, unease blankets Marian's pale face. Courage surfaces on Ahmik's dark skin. I think he looks like a warrior going into battle. I start the ritual. I fill every crevice of my lungs with the cool air. Now I've got to exhale forcefully. Dust flies on the table. Okay, one more suck of the still air. I'll just hold my breath as long as . . . I order my eyelids to close. The secret door into the past opens.

"It's a pirate ship with three masts. I see the skull and crossbones. The sails are ripped apart. Waves . . . crashing over the ship. A mast snaps. Someone is pulling a thick line. Oh, he's gone. The sea took him. I hear screams.Another wave crashes over the bow of the ship. It's on its side. It's breaking apart. It's sinking. Men jump overboard. Waves, tall as a barn. Thunder, lightning, screaming, lots of screaming." Everything stops. I feel beads of sweat rolling down my forehead and into my eyes. I scrunch them tighter. I feel my chin collapse on my chest. My head moves in time with my breathing. I hear Ahmik and Marian's voices, but they're far away. Yes, they're far away. Slowly I try to open my eyes. Ahmik. Marian. They're here . . . right in front of me.

"Did I say anything?" My saucer eyes go from Marian to Ahmik while they sit frozen.

"Peter, you look like nothing happened. You must be kidding." Ahmik's comment surprises me. Again I hear him ask me, "Are you kidding us?"

"I don't remember anything. What happened? Did I say anything interesting?"

Marian looks dazed, but she's still capable of a comment, "Peter, you described everything as if you were there. You told us about a three-mast pirate ship. It sank. Don't you remember?"

Ahmik adds, "The sea washed a man overboard. Men jumped into the ocean. Giant waves tore the ship in half. You even said the waves were as tall as a barn."

"I did?" This is so strange. My face must show how surprised I am. They're telling me I saw all these things happening, but I don't remember.

"Yes," Ahmik insists, "you have to remember. You have to tell your father what you can do when you hold the box. The images brought by the eagle vision will reveal an unsolved mystery. I saw how the eagle eye worked with another member of my clan. It will happen with you."

I'm not ready to tell my father about the images. I need more scenes. If my father's story mirrors the images I see, then . . . the two events are the same.

"Marian, it's important that we know the whole story. Do you think you can write it down when I say it?"

"You talk too fast, Peter. I can't write that fast." She thinks for a moment then continues, "When you wake up . . . I'm not sure what to call it, but when you stop dreaming – yes, that's it. After you dream, Ahmik and I can work together and write down what we remember."

"That'll work." Ahmik has an uneasy look on his face. "Don't worry Ahmik. You just have to tell what you remember, and Marian will do the writing, okay?"

"We'll try, Peter." Marian lifts her chin and flutters her eyelashes.

Excitement fills every corner of the shed. Marian wants to practice taking notes while I talk. I get impatient when Marian doesn't write fast enough or when she tries to make her letters and spelling perfect.

"If you're going to rush me, maybe you need to find someone else who can do it faster." Oh, oh . . . she has her hands on her hips.

"We can wait," I mumble. I need her. We really don't want to do this without you." She calms down moving her head gently side to side and up and down as her shoulders relax.

"Peter, my Ma says I've been spending more time here than at home, and my chores aren't finished. Yesterday she said I can't come over here for a week.

"Me too, Peter. My father has work I must do for the clan." Ahmik lowers his eyes to the floor waiting for my answer.

"It's okay. We don't want our parents to keep us from getting together, so . . . I'll see you later."

Outside the shed, Patches waits for me. "Oh, Patches, I wish you could see what I see. It's so exciting." His long tail beats his sides.

"Sometimes I think you understand every word I say." To let me know how he's feeling, Patches leaps into the air. "You're happy, aren't you?"

*   *   *

Five days pass. I haven't held the box even once. If I did, Marian and Ahmik would kill me. Not peering into the past makes me jumpy.

"Hello, hello. Where are you, Peter." From outside, Marian's voice makes me smile. Today it's like music. Other times, when she's angry, she sounds like a witch. I hate that voice.

The door squeaks open, Marian's smiling face looks into the room. "There you are Peter. You aren't doing anything without us, are you?"

"I didn't start without you. Now that we're together, we're ready. Wonder what I'll see this time." Marian is about to speak but feels Ahmik poke her arm. Her lips part and then snap shut.

"I'm ... ready. You both have to listen very carefully so you get all the details. Right?" My partners nod agreement. I take my place at the table facing the small silver window to the past. Marian and Ahmik squeeze together on the narrow wooden bench. Their hands are tightly joined. I remember what I did the last time I looked into the past. Breathe, exhale, breathe. It begins. My eyelashes tightly mesh together

"What? Where am I? I . . . I'm on a dock. A schooner. A British flag snaps in the wind. Workers push barrels and carry baskets up the ramp. They put the cargo below deck. Two people. Fog. I think they're getting ready to board that ship." I watch. Minutes tick by. I say nothing. I feel my eyeballs rolling behind my eyelids. I wonder who these people are.

Another flash. "Yes, I see them. A strong wind is tugging at the woman's long blue cloak. White fur around the hood. The older grey-haired gentleman has a beard. The lady's turning to face him. Oh, my. She's young. Maybe he's her father. They're going up the ramp. The wind snatches her hood from her head. She's soooo beautiful. Sun-gold curls frame her face. I've never . . . wait . . . the older man is giving her something. She has both hands out to take it. I can't see what it is. It's hidden between her white gloves. Now I see it. It's a blue purse decorated with little pearls. He's holding it open. Oh, no, I don't believe it. It can't be . . . it's the box, our silver box. She's putting it in the purse. Her wrist goes into the loop. Now he's giving her a hug."

I open my eyes. Marian is trying to appear calm, but she's scratching her arms here and there.

"What's the matter with you?" I ask.

"I guess all the suspense made my skin itch. Peter, I have to know who these people are, where they're going, and who this girl is. My heart can't stand still. I feel like my face is as red as a beet. Am I red, Peter?" She takes two gulps, swallows hard, closes her eyes and calms herself.

Crazy ideas and possible answers to her questions pop in and out of my brain. Fear and excitement rush from the soles of my feet to the top of my head. My scalp tingles. I scratch my head. Marian laughs.

Ahmik stares at both of us. "Be calm, Marian, Peter needs your help."

* * *

A knock on the door. My eyes jerk open. Ahmik and Marian are on their feet looking surprised. Patches who was asleep in the corner is already at the door.

"Grrrrrrr." A low growl. A stiff tail. Ears straight up.

"What is it, boy?" Another knock.

"Ruff, ruff." A deep loud bark. That's a warning.

"Who is it?" I ask. No one answers. I crack open the door just enough to see who is outside. Doggie squeezes his nose alongside me. I grab his collar and hold him back.

"Grrrrrrrrrr." The low deep growl makes the man step back.

We stare at each other. The man's old and shabby. His dark eyes are fixed on me. I know this man. He's the one I saw on the property. He's the one I saw in town. What's he doing here?

"My folks are in the cabin. You'll have to talk to them if you're looking for work." Two squinting eyes shoot through me. Suddenly, the man's gaze searches over my head in the direction of the table. Ahmik and Marian are statues in front of the table. Their bodies hide the box. His foot pushes against the door. I've got the edge of the door refusing to let the man push it open. I put my foot behind the door. This door isn't going anywhere.

The stranger wants to see what's here. He's definitely looking for something. He steps away from the door, turns and starts toward the cabin. I slam the door, lean against it and whisper, "I think he's looking for the box." I move to the table and pick up the silver container.

"I don't know what's going on, Peter, but we better retell what you saw and correct what we wrote, or we won't remember it. It's unbelievable. Wait until you hear what you said." Ahmik and Marian take turns retelling the scene about the British schooner, about the beauty wrapped in a cloak and the bearded older man. Ahmik stops. He begins again, "The man could be her father. He gave her something, then he gave her a beaded purse and when she opened her hands . . . Peter, Peter . . . there it was . . . our silver box."

"Who is she? Did I say anything about who these people are? Where was this dock?" Questions shoot like arrows between us. Then, quiet.

Marian, never one to enjoy silence, is the first to break the silence, "We can't answer your questions. You didn't say any of those things. The only detail that can give us a clue is that the ship was flying a British flag, and the people were dressed in very fine clothes. I think they were nobility."

A worried Ahmik asks, "Who was that man at the door, Peter, and what did he want?"

CHAPTER TWELVE

"It's time. I must tell my father about the box, about what I saw and about the stranger. I hope he tells us about shipwrecks off our coast. Maybe everything I saw really happened." My friends tail after me with frown lines etched on their foreheads, jaws locked and heads slightly dipped. I'm just the opposite. I walk tall, spine straight and chest high. My lips form a thin line no thicker than a blade of grass. I hope my eyes show how curious, how courageous and how determined I am.

"Let's go in together," I say. We'll make a bigger impression. Like a good team of horses, we prance together into the cabin. In a heartbeat, we're next to Pa. We wait for him to notice. I can't find my voice. I shiver. I can almost hear my nerve jangling like Christmas bells.

"Pa, I - we - I have to know about shipwrecks and we have to tell you something."

I watch Marian and Ahmik. They're slightly behind me. Worry colors their faces. Bet my father thinks we're all in trouble.

"I think you'd better tell me what this is all about."

"Pa ..." Before I can continue, a frown creeps over Pa's face. I don't know for sure how that frown when fully developed, makes me stammer like a three-year-old. I lace my fingers together and plant my hands on the worn wooden table. My fast breathing has no end. The story unravels. "Pa, you remember how I had a healing with the Abamela Shaman. What I didn't explain is that I have the eye of an eagle."

"What does that mean, Peter?" Pa shifts side to side in his chair. My voice signals concern. That sound stings my father. Pa's body tilts forward in an effort to catch every word.

"Go on, Peter. Tell me everything. I mean everything." From the look on Pa's face, I know he's giving me his full attention.

"This is how it happens, Pa." I lick my lips, suck the dry air and go on. "I close my eyes, I watch, then tell what I see. Ahmik and Marian listen, and when I wake up, Marian has written it down."

Marian holds out a piece of paper with her neatly written letters. "This is one of our papers, Mr. Poppin." Pa takes the paper from Marian. He squints. His narrow eyes creep from top to bottom.

Like a storm cloud, I open up and pour all the visions into the warm cabin air – the pirate ship sinking, the beautiful woman receiving a gift. The images churn and swirl around Pa's head like a hurricane. His eyes narrow to slits, his cheeks move in and out as he grinds his teeth. Pa struggles to absorb what he hears.

"The most important thing, Pa, is holding the box, closing my eyes and then ... it's all there."

"Peter, what do you mean, it's all there?"

"Pa, it's the truth. The past, Pa, the past is all there. I see it all. It's silver, Pa, the box is silver with fancy letters on the top."

I run to the shed and fetch the box. My hands tremble as I set it in front of my father's weathered hands, almost too rough to touch such an object.

"Peter." Pa's frown deepens above his eyebrows as one finger inches down Marian's paper. "I don't understand how it's possible. I mean ... how can you see the past?"

For the next hour, Pa tells of a pirate ship sinking off the coast.

"For years, Peter, bits, and pieces of the wreckage washed up on the shore. We'll ask other menfolk in town. They'll remember more about it. I do remember something about a British schooner."

I flinch realizing what his words could mean. One of Marian's high-pitched squeaks punctuates the tension-filled room.

"Oh, Pa . . ." Words trip over themselves in my head. Jumbled words. I open my mouth so they can pour out and make sense, but they don't.

"What is it, son?"

"Everything m . . . m . . . matches. Sweat covers my palms. My hands tremble. I want more visions, but my father has other ideas.

"That's enough for tonight. It's dark, and you two have to get home. We'll talk again. Ahmik and Marian head home. I can't help but think about Ahmik. What was he thinking when Pa talked about the pirates? Marian's eyes were as giant as a full moon as she listened.

Before Ahmik is out the door, he turns to me, "You've got to tell your Pa about the stranger who came to the shed tonight." He's almost down the steps when he comes back and whispers to me, "You've got to ask your Pa to keep your secret – our clan secret." My nodding head tells him I know.

Marian can't meet us until the end of the week. When we meet, her first words are, "What have you been doing? What did I miss? What visions did you have? I do wish you had waited for me." I spin around, and squint in her direction, "We did."

Marian's body begins to collapse. "Sor . . . ry. I just thought . . . oh, never mind." I catch her eye and let my dimples show. She relaxes.

The end of the second day finds us learning about pirates who made off with jewels, chests filled with fine clothes and boxes of gold coins. Passengers were not harmed. The young woman continued on to Portsmouth with nothing but the clothes on her back. I discover the woman's name. It's Lady Jane Emerald. The box has 'LJE' – Lady Jane Emerald, and she's here in Maine.

The new details fascinate my father. He says, "It's a puzzle. Don't worry, Peter, others will help us solve the puzzle."

Setting his jaw, Pa shows his determination, "I'll call the town together and find out what they know."

"Pa?" A question forms in my mind, but I hesitate. Pa shoots a questioning look in my direction. "Pa, you have to . . ." With each word, I resolve to keep the Shaman's ceremony a secret. "You must not tell anyone the Shaman healed me, and they can't know I have the eye of an eagle. They wouldn't - they couldn't understand."

"What can we tell them?" My father shakes his head trying to order his tangled thoughts. "I've got it. Leave it to me. Don't worry. I promise not to say anything about the healing."

CHAPTER THIRTEEN

Townspeople are milling around the front of the church when our family arrives. Dr. Barrett greets Pa with a cordial handshake and tips his hat at Ma.

"What's this all about, Tom?" He stares down noticing that I'm not wearing the patch. "And how are you, Peter. I'm surprised you're not wearing your patch." I want to tell him that I can see, but I don't have time to answer. We move away leaving the doctor with many questions unanswered. Ma's found her friends inside the church.

Standing tall, Pa looks like a person with a mission.

"I'll explain. I have something important to tell everyone. Please, go inside." As they enter the little white church, there are questions shot like arrows that are trying to get into Pa's head. Everyone wants an answer. I'm so keyed up, I can't sit still so I pick a spot in the back of the church and stand against the wall. My legs jitter. I see Ma turn around looking for me. Our eyes meet and she nods.

Pa raises his arms. Apprehension and fear melt into murmurs and end in silence. A frown of concentration wrinkles Pa's forehead. Staring at the crowd, doubt thunders through my mind.

At last with a deep breath, Pa begins, "My friends and neighbors, I called you here this afternoon to talk about two things. First, shipwrecks along our coast and second, the strangers in town."

"Why do you want to know about shipwrecks, Tom?" a grizzled man who is in the last row shouts out.

Pa thinks quickly, "Miss Prim is going to do a play about this area for the fall festival, and she needs all the information we can give her."

Then he answers the question with a question. "Does anyone know about a pirate attack a few years back?"

"Sure do, Tom." A red-bearded man gets to his feet. He brushes his forehead with his sleeve before going on. "My father knew a man who worked on the schooners that sailed from England. A young woman was on that ship. Her father was a duke. No, I think it was a . . ." A low voice rings out, "He was a Lord, Lord Emerald. He had something to do with Parliament."

Quiet rises to the rafters. Everyone, except me, is breathing in unison. My mind wraps around the idea that it might be true. I want to shout, but my throat traps my voice.

"Can anyone tell me who the girl was?" Pa aska, his eyes scanning the crowd.

Mr. Hancock, the blacksmith, volunteers, "Her name was Jane, Lady Jane and her father sent her to Portsmouth. A pirate ship attacked them and took everything." Gasps break the quiet.

The blacksmith goes on, "Same pirate ship caught in a gale. Torn apart, it was ripped to shreds. Everything went down. It's told that some pirates swam ashore and travelled north."

A timid voice somewhere in the middle of the crowd says, "They got what they deserved. Amen, I say."

Pa looks over the crowd now whispering among themselves. His eyes meet mine.

"Peter, I want you to tell our friends what you found and what you know about the strangers." I'm shocked. I can't move. What's my father doing? Pa motions to me to stand.

"Come up here, Peter." I'm on my feet, but they're clamped to the floor. Body stiff. I shuffle forward until I'm face to face with my father. My back is to everyone who came to hear Pa's message.

"Pa," I whisper so no one can hear, "I don't know what to say." My voice shudders. My hands quiver. The walls of the tiny church move in pressing the air against me so it's too tight to breathe in. Slowly I turn to face a sea of brown, blue, green, and grey eyes – all staring out of tension filled faces. I look once at the crowd then make my eyes find a spot on the back wall. Words drip slowly, like molasses, from my tongue.

The story unfolds until my trembling hand pulls the silver box out of my pocket. It sits on the palm of my hand shining at the townsfolk. Ooooooos and aaaaaahs escape from half-open mouths.

"Have you opened it, Peter?" someone hollers from the middle of the group.

"No . . . not yet." One by one, the crowd gets quiet. They gawk at the box.

"Peter tell us about the man. Tell us everything. We should know."

"I think . . ." Pa jumps in, "I believe the strangers in town are looking for Peter's box. They could be pirates who survived the shipwreck." The room ceases to be still, it buzzes, alive with hundreds of bees whose hive had been disturbed. The hum grows and grows until I cover my ears. Dr. Barrett is on his feet, "I didn't think anything about it." The crowd quiets. "Those same two men asked me a lot of questions about the boy who had the accident. I thought they were just curious. Now I realize they were trying to find out where you lived, Peter. I'm sorry, Tom, I didn't tell you." A rush of surprise rises from the louder voices.

"What's in the box, Tom? Yeah, open the box, Tom." Loud voices clamor about the box and its secret contents. Several men, on their feet, strain their necks to get a good look. I glance over at my mother. She's still. All I see are her blinking eyes. The more nervous she is, the faster she blinks.

"We'll open the box, but . . . the box and its contents must be returned to its owner," Pa states in a matter-of-fact tone. The room takes on a grey tone with somber faces bobbing right then left to get a glimpse of what is about to happen. At least I didn't have to reveal the visions and my healing. A rock settles in the bottom of my stomach. A sigh almost escapes, but it has second thoughts and stays where it is.

CHAPTER FOURTEEN

ear begins to tumble around in my chest. I'm not sure what I'm afraid about. Everyone waits. No one gets up to leave the crowded church. I find myself wondering if the visions will stop once the box is open. Is this the only thing I was supposed to see in the past? Maybe I shouldn't open it.

Pa is at my side, "Peter, are you all right? Did you hear me? I want you to open the box." You can use my knife. Think of the box as a fine piece of wood. Imagine you're carving it."

"Thanks, Pa, but I'll use my knife. I trust it." I find a barely-visible seam that locks the contents inside. The tip of my knife makes its first mark. Rotating the box, the knife circles around and around. With each rotation, a deep channel takes shape.

"Try it now, Peter," someone calls out.

My knife never jumps out of its groove. One more turn, and then it should open. The knife follows the trough. I try to jiggle the lid. It budges. My lungs suck at the charged air. Eyes, are unable to leave the object. One more forceful jerk and the lid jumps off the box, landing on the church floor. The sound of the silver lid hitting the floor breaks the quiet, but no one moves. I can't go after the lid.

A gem, a jewel – I've never seen anything like it. My eyes blink and blink again. My jaw finds the floor. When Pa sees what I'm looking at, he can't find his voice. Neither can I. Boy, Ma is going to be surprised.

A deep voice breaks the stillness, "Peter, what is it? Show us what it is."

I stare into the box. I close my eyes expecting the gem to disappear, but when I open them, it's still there shining its brilliance into my eyes.

"Show us, show us, show us," echoes off the walls.

My thumb and index finger slip around the jewel. Icy cold. I lift the jewel high above my head.

"An emerald," someone cries out. "An emerald that belongs to Lady Jane Emerald. Green . . . green as . . . green as . . . it's . . ."

"It's special," I murmur as I soak in its lush color and its perfect lines and angles.

"Can we hold it, Tom?" The question snatches Pa out of his dream into reality. He has to do something so everyone is satisfied. Men and women, boys and girls are on their feet trying to get a look.

"Sit down. Everyone sit down, please. You'll all get a chance to see the jewel, but you have to sit down." Bodies continue to pop up and down, swaying first one way then another. Murmurs, whispers, sounds formed by lips smother the stillness.

I can't imagine what will happen next, but my stomach does a cartwheel, a definite warning sign. I can't let anything happen to this emerald. Suddenly I need Marian. My eyes gallop around the room searching for her. I see her. She's holding her mother's hand. Her eyes flashing. Her cheeks glowing. Our eyes collide. Her smile reassures me.

"We'll pass around the box so everyone can see the jewel and . . ." Pa's voice is once again strong. It fills every inch of the church.

"Can we touch it, Tom?"

"Yes, but very carefully," Pa says in a very loud voice so everyone hears him. I cringe. My muscles pull against each other. I have to obey Pa. I have to believe the emerald will be safe. Like a slug, I pull my body along the floor to the man at the end of the front row. I rest the silver box in the center of the over-size burly hand that looks like a claw waiting for an insect to land and be snatched out of its existence. The stone-faced man gapes at the beauty. His cracked finger gently touches the jewel. He grins. He lifts it up. He seems unwilling to let it go. Then, he puts the gem back in the box and passes it to the next person. Each person explores, then praises the treasure.

"Unbelievable!"

"Must be worth a king's ransom!"

"Can't believe my eyes."

What matters is that they'll all experience the precious gemstone. Normal somber-lined faces light up with cheerfulness, warmth, and pleasure. When my Ma gets to hold the stone, a little gasp slips between her lips. Her eyes sparkle and a stare has replaced the blinking. My lips tilt up in a full grin. Pa's eyes declare his satisfaction.

Daylight disappears. After holding the stone, Ma and some of the women leave to prepare the evening meal. A group of men linger behind.

"What are we going to do now, Tom" one neighbor asks quietly.

Pa is more serious now. "We need a plan to protect the stone and to catch anyone who might try to steal the object. Peter, you'll be part of this plan."

CHAPTER FIFTEEN

Excitement leaves the church charged with a nervous energy. The remaining ladies are fidgeting with shawls and children. Men are turning around, looking over their shoulders and muttering to themselves. No one can stand still. Comments about capturing a possible thief travel among the men.

I've got to make sure the emerald is returned to Lady Jane. She's the one in the vision. She's the rightful owner of the jewel. One scheme flows into another. The men toss around ideas about how to trick the would-be thieves. How long will it take them to choose one?

Pa is on his feet. "Gentlemen, gentlemen, quiet down. The plan you choose must be simple and easy to put into action. We can use the festival that is planned at the school as a setting." Heads nod and murmurs of 'uh-huh' along with a few 'ayes' are heard from the crowd.

Before I know it, I'm standing next to Pa. "Ahem, ahem," I need their attention. Everyone stops talking and looks at me. "We'll put up signs announcing the festival. I'll read you the words we'll use on the signs.

ON DISPLAY AT THE FESTIVAL
OLD PIECES OF SHIPWRECKED PIRATE SHIPS
DISCOVERED TREASURE
THE SILVER BOX
THE EMERALD
COME SEE FOR YOURSELF

If the strangers are after the jewel, they'll be sure to come, and we'll catch them. All of us kids at school can make the signs."

I overhear the sheriff telling Pa, "The two men you're asking about live on the outskirts of town in a small boarding house."

Pa asks, "When do they come to town?"

"Only when they need supplies. They don't come for anything else. Really don't know much about them." The sheriff wrinkles his brow and Pa's concern darkens his face.

* * *

Pa and I leave early to get to the store. Patches comes along. It's quiet in town today. Usually, there are men on horseback, wagons loaded with hay rattling down Main Street, even kids running around, but there's none of that going on. Everyone must be getting ready for the festival tomorrow. We've only had two ladies buying groceries this morning. Usually, we have at least six by this time.

"Pa, what if those men don't come to the festival?

"They will, Peter. I'm almost certain they will. If they're the least bit interested in getting their hands on that emerald, the signs around town will convince them this is their opportunity. Don't you worry. They'll be there. It's important that we, men, are prepared for anything that happens." Just as Pa finishes his sentence, one of the strangers walks into the store.

Patches leaps to his feet. His body alert. Ears up, tail out. Sniff, sniff. He samples the air trying to learn about the stranger. He watches. I think he recognizes the man.

"Good morning, can I help you?" Pa's voice is outgoing and welcoming. I busy myself bundling small sacks of flour for those customers who only want small quantities. Pa says it's good to give the customers what they want, but right now, I'm more interested to learn about the man who came into the store. I don't think I can call them strangers anymore. First, he and his friend were on the bluff, then on our property. I'm sure this is the one who asked Pa for work. I think it's time to ask what his name is.

"Hi, I'm Peter. This is my father's store. What's your name?" Patches comes over to my side – still looking alert. My father drops the twine he was wrapping around a bundle onto the counter, picks it up and walks toward us.

"Howdy, Peter. I'm Ben, and I need a dozen eggs and some milk – two quarts will do."

"I'll be happy to help you with that," Pa says. He goes to the back room for the eggs. My eyes swivel sideways to see him. I watch Ben's every move. I study his face. He doesn't look like a thief. But, I'm not sure what a thief would look like anyway. Ben mills around the store and stops in front of one of our signs. My heart knocks against my ribs. Doggie walks up behind him and sniffs his pants. He must think everything is okay. He takes his place in the corner of the store.

Pa's back with a dozen eggs. He puts them on the counter. "You're new in town, aren't you?" Ben looks around the store. His eyes settle on Pa.

Pa continues, "I saw you and your friend in front of the bank last week. Where's your friend?"

If Pa asks too many questions, he might wonder why Pa is so curious. I scrunch up my face and hope he sees me. Maybe he'll get my message.

No answer, just a little grunt. Pa strides over to the sign on the wall near the front window.

"Are you and your friend going to the festivities this Sunday? Children practiced their presentation about the history of our setlement for weeks. They're mighty proud. It'll be a great picnic with home cooked food and music. There'll be dancing too. Won't cost you anything. All you have to do is show up after noon." The stranger is beginning to look uneasy. His left shoulder twitches and he begins to chew on the inside of his cheek.

I knew it. Too many questions. Now maybe he won't come.

The tall, thin man doesn't look Pa in the eye . . . he just mumbles, "How much do I owe?"

"That'll be seventy cents."

He puts the coins on the counter and shoves them toward Pa. With his bundle, he walks toward the door. Not even a good-bye. He's probably anxious to get away from all the questions. Then he stops right in front of the colorful sign. His right index finger traces the word 'found'. Then he's gone. Is he really a thief? Is he an old pirate who attacked and robbed the ship that carried Lady Jane? Is he after the jewel?

Pa goes to the window. His hands are on his hips, lips pushed forward, brow wrinkled. His eyes follow the man down the street.

"Pa, Patches didn't seem to like that man much."

"Maybe there's a reason, Peter." Then he adds, "Not too friendly, was he?" I nod wanting to tell Pa that he did too much talking, but I decide it's best to leave it.

* * *

This is the day we've all been waiting for. Miss Prim had us rehearse our parts for the history play a hundred times. It was probably more like twenty, but it seemed like a hundred. Our signs are all around town. The men in town know where they have to be and what they have to do to guard the jewel and to catch the thieves if they even come. The plan is in motion.

The fiddler strikes up a note and the fun begins. A few people polka around the yard. Dust flies around their feet. If they're not dancing, they're clapping to the rhythm of the music. All the women arrive with dishes whose aromas make my mouth water. They place them on the makeshift tables the men built. Many neighbors brought their dogs. Patches and the others run after each other. I wonder what Patches will do if the strangers arrive. I'm so nervous my stomach has humming birds flitting around inside.

Pa and I take turns greeting neighbors at the entrance to the schoolyard. When another giant pot of yummy smelling food arrives, my empty stomach makes strange noises. When Pa walks over to take my place my hand traces a circle around my belly. "Pa, are we going to eat soon?"

"After the performance. A little after two, Peter." I frown. My stomach erupts into grumbles.

"What time is it now, Pa? Pa takes out his pocket watch, peers down at it and says, "Almost one-thirty. Now, get, Peter. Go find your friends."

"I'll be dead by two, Pa." Pa's eyes twinkle. His chuckle makes me laugh. I twist my mouth into a half smile, turn away and head toward Marian, who's helping the ladies arrange the dishes. Ma smiles and giggles with the other ladies.

"Are they here yet, Peter?" Marian spins around looking in all directions.

"Not yet, Marian. Maybe they're not going to come," I say in a somber voice. "Pa asked too many questions. I think he scared them away. Maybe they're not even in town anymore."

"Don't be silly, Peter. Of course they'll come." Marian is as certain as Pa. How can they be so sure? I want to believe they'll come, but I have my doubts.

"Have you seen Ahmik, Marian? I've been so busy I didn't see him come in. He told me he hoped his father would come. It would be good for Standing Bear to meet some of the townspeople. Pa would like it if the Indians and our people could work together. That would be good, and maybe more Indian children would come to school." Marian watches me.

"Peter, can I answer your question?" Marian gives me one of her pouty looks.

"Sorry, Marian, when I'm nervous, my mouth has to move. What did I ask you?" I'm ashamed I don't remember.

"You wanted to know if I had seen Ahmik. Remember?" Marian raises her eyebrows. "To answer your question, Peter – no, I haven't seen him."

"Marian, I feel pretty bad that Ahmik didn't get to hold the jewel the night we showed it."

"Don't worry, Peter. He'll see it and hold it today. It'll be a special time just for him." She smiles and inside I know she's right.

I look toward the gate hoping to see Ahmik, instead, I'm surprised to see Ben and his friend – I've got to find out his name.

"They're here, Marian, you and Pa were right, they came. I'll see you later, Marian." I get to Pa just as they enter the yard.

"Welcome, welcome. Glad you came, Ben." That's the way Pa's been greeting all the guests. A broad smile covers his face.

"This is my friend, Stanley," Ben says softly. They don't wait for Pa to answer. They nod and pass. No handshake – strange. They seem to be in a hurry. I don't think they want to answer more questions. I watch as they mill around glancing, not once, but three times at the little church where a sign over the door announces 'See the Treasure Inside.' My eyes stay glued to them. If they make a move in the direction of the church, I'll be after them.

Right after Ben and Stanley arrive, Ahmik and Standing Bear near the gate. I'm glad they're here. After all, Ahmik had an important role in the story of the emerald.

My father grins at them both. His right-hand moves quickly to shake hands with Standing Bear whose hand connects in lightning speed with Pa's.

"Peter, I'd like you to meet Standing Bear. He's been my Abamela trading partner for about five years." I already know that from my visit to the village, but I don't remember telling Pa about Standing Bear's part in the healing. I smile.

"Would you take my place greeting people?" Pa is already walking away as I answer. He and Standing Bear continue their conversation.

"Sure, Pa," I call after him. Ahmik stays for a second runs over to Marian and brings her back. The three of us now have the job of greeting new arrivals.

"Don't forget to smile," I tell my friends who already have grins on their lips. "Got to make everyone feel welcome."

Do Marian and Ahmik feel like I do – nervous? My nerves clink together. All I can think is how dangerous it is to stop someone who might want to steal the gem.

"Peter, are they here? Did you see them? Where did they go?" Marian's eyes dart around the yard now full of townspeople. "We have to keep an eye on them," she insists.

"I'm not sure why they didn't shake hands with Pa. They left him standing there with his hand out. Not even a smile. They just started walking around." Marian and I look at each other shaking our heads left and right.

"That wasn't too polite, was it?" Marian's curls jump around.

"No, it wasn't," I agree.

"We have to help with all the food," Marian reminds us.

"I want to help, Marian, Ahmik says. What do we have to do? Explain, Marian." I'm pleased that Ahmik wants to help.

"I have a lot to tell you, Ahmik. I haven't seen you and so much has happened." Ahmik frowns for a long time. I tell him about the church, opening the box and the plan the men put together.

"You have to help us guard the jewel." As I talk his eyes grow wider and he seems to grow taller.

I put my hand on his shoulder. "Ahmik, it's super important that we know exactly what Ben and Stanley are doing. You're in charge of watching them. Make sure you tell me right away if they head toward the church. Okay?"

"I can do that, Peter." Ahmik looks around the yard, picks out a place to stand.

"I'll stand next to the last table, Peter. I can see everything from there. They won't get by me, Peter. You'll know if they move."

"Good, Ahmik. Now, Marian, what do I do?" Marian smiles ready to put me in charge of something.

"Well," she says with her hands straightening her apron, "When the women need something you can run off and fetch it." I'm just about ready to ask another question when I hear my name.

"Peter, can you bring us two of those wooden buckets from around the back of the church?"

"Sure, Mrs. Healy. I'll get them for you." I go around the side of the church. Marian skips after me.

"I want to go with you, Peter," she yells.

"I'm getting two buckets for Mrs. Healy. Didn't you hear her ask me?" Marian frowns.

"No, I didn't. Anyway, you better hurry up. Don't keep her waiting." I'm about to say something when I see she's grinning. She's just teasing me. I'll get her later.

The music is loud, but above it we hear the cry, "Eeeeeeeee Eeeeeeeee." The eagle, my eagle is straight overhead. We freeze. We tilt our heads back shading our eyes. It dips, it dives, it sketches a small tight circle, then another – bigger and bigger. It swoops down. It's so close I look into its eyes. My mouth opens to make a sound, but only air escapes. My heart beats to the tempo of the eagle's flapping wings. Then, with one mighty motion, the powerful eagle flies straight up becoming smaller and smaller. We stand hypnotized then bolt to the yard where all the people are on their feet pointing at the disappearing bird. The music has stopped.

"Ah-Oooooooooow, Ah-Oooooooooooow, ooow, ooow" the dogs call out to the great eagle. They're all answering his call. Then quiet.

"I can't believe it," one of the ladies who's in Ma's quilting group shouts.

"I've never seen an eagle do that. What does it mean?" another adds.

"It's so beautiful. Like a dance. Why is it here? Why is it here? The question goes around in my head. I know the answer. Everyone else can only guess.

I look around for Ahmik. He's exactly where he said he would be with his eyes glued on Ben and Stanley who are standing with the others. Ben's mouth hangs open. I bet he's never seen anything like that. Ahmik turns to find me. Our eyes lock. A tiny jerk of his head lets me know that he saw it. So far, nothing has happened. Maybe they're not the thieves. Could it be that someone else is going to try to steal the emerald?

Lots of questions. Few answers. Murmurs along with oos and ahs mix with laughter and mumbles. My eyes stare at the spot where the eagle disappeared. Ahmik runs over to me.

"Peter, it's a sign. The eagle is talking to you," says Ahmik in a hushed tone.

"Do you think we should explain the eagle to anyone?" I ask.

"I . . ." Before I go on, I remember Mrs. Healy and the water. A voice behind us asks, "Are you going to bring me those buckets or not?" Ahmik runs back to his spot, and I run to the buckets and bring them to her.

I find my father in the schoolyard. "Pa, did you see it? What do you think?" He takes a deep breath and whispers, "Must be a good sign."

Pa had asked several men to guard the jewel. I remember Pa said someone would be standing guard outside the backdoor of the church, and there would always be someone watching inside the church. Everyone would take turns – even some of the older boys. Pa wanted to make sure no one would steal the gem.

Every once in a while a few people move up the steps, go into the church and in a few minutes come out. None of the guards have come running out screaming, 'They've got the jewel.' For now it's safe and for now, Ahmik is still watching the two suspected thieves.

"Ahmik, you can stop watching for a couple of minutes. We want to take a look at the jewel. Come with us," I say leading the way to where we displayed the emerald.

I walk up the steps and stop at the door. Ahmik bumps into me. "Where's Marian?" We wait.

"I'm here, I'm here," she gasps. We enter the cold space. Marian shivers. "Look, Peter, how beautiful." She's already standing in front of the table while Ahmik and I seem glued to a spot a couple feet away. I look to the left and see Jacob, one of the senior boys standing watch. He tilts his head toward me.

We move closer. Now we see what she's talking about. A special table has been set with a starched tablecloth and bunches of wild flowers. A large hand-made doily, one like Ma crochets, is draped over something to form a platform. The gleaming silver box perches atop it. The lid rests to the right of the box where the initials LJE announces the owner. The dark green gemstone appears to float in the box. Marian lets out a little puff of air. Almik's lips look like he's saying, 'Wow' but no sound comes from his lips. My eyes gawk at the stone. Its magic, its power captures me. My heart that was beating so fast is perfectly still. I know the gem is being kept safe. Everyone is doing a good job.

"Let's go. We have to get back to watching outside," I whisper. The three of us tiptoe out of the church. From the emerald's silent beauty into a noisy celebration. Music, food, dancing and the eagle's visit have everyone celebrating. The crowd is in motion except for the outsiders who sit alone in the shade of the oak. They're very still. Not making a move. Are they planning on getting into the church while we're all busy with the recitations? Maybe they think no one is guarding the back door. They'll be surprised, won't they?

We'll have to be very careful. I know there are some men who volunteered to watch at performance time because they don't have children in the play. I think Pa thought of everything when he planned this.

Clang, clang, clang.

Pa strikes the bottom of a metal pot with a large wooden spoon. It makes enough noise to get everyone's attention.

"Ladies and gentlemen," Pa begins, "Miss Prim is going to lead the children in their recitation. Will all the children take their places?"

"Marian, Ahmik, we've got to watch them. I'm certain they're about to make their move."

"Who?" I can't believe Marian is asking 'who?'

"You know who, Marian."

"I thought you wanted us to watch someone in the recitation, Peter." Annoyance colors every word.

"Sorry, Marian. I should have been more specific." Everyone is on edge. We're all nervous. Have to calm down.

"This would be the perfect time for someone to sneak into the church and . . . . I don't get time to finish my sentence. Marian is already nodding. She understands my message.

Miss Prim steps to the front of the little makeshift platform. "Now, we're going to hear from Peter Poppin. He'll tell us about the Abamela clan, our Indian neighbors to the north.

"Thank you, Miss Prim." I take a deep breath. I hope I remember everything I practiced. "The Abamela clans are our neighbors. They've lived on this land for hundreds and hundreds of years. They are friendly." I find Ahmik in the crowd. "My very good friend, Ahmik, is a member of the clan. His father, Standing Bear, and my Pa are trading partners." Everyone smiles as I point to Ahmik. "The Abamela are very clever. They have two wigwams, one covered with one layer of birch bark for the warm months and one covered with hides for the winter. They're comfortable all the time. They hunt and fish and grow most of their own food. Ahmik and Standing Bear are over there with my Pa." Everyone turns their head to find them. Standing Bear nods. "Thank you for coming." I leave the platform and hope that the jewel is still safe.

Boy, am I glad that's over. Everyone is clapping. Miss Prim's lips stretch across her face. And . . . the best part is no one made a move to get up the steps and into the church. I've been watching, and they're still hidden in the shade. Maybe we're wrong. Maybe they're just passersby trying to find a town to settle in. Maybe no one is trying to steal the stone.

As I look over toward the doors to the church, two couples and their children are walking up the steps of the church. Our mystery men, Ben and Stanley are on the move. Oh, oh. They're following those families.

Ahmik pokes me. "Peter, do you see what's happening?" Marian is already in motion toward the stairs.

"Wait, Marian, wait for us." I grab her arm. "What are you doing?"

"Peter, it's happening. The jewel is going to disappear if we don't do something." Panic paints Marian's words a bright red.

I know Marian could be right. "Marian, we're got to stay calm." The men are walking slowly, very casually. If I hurry, I can pass them. The next thing I know I'm on the top step, Marian and Ahmik trailing. Got to act now. I spin around, smile, and ask, "Are you enjoying the picnic?" I can't think of anything else to say. How dumb is that?

"Yes, it's good," the tall one answers. His friend taps the toe of his boot on the planks.

"I'm Peter Poppin, I met you in Pa's grocery in town. These are my friends, Marian, and Ahmik."

"What's your name?" Marian jumps into the conversation. I can't believe it. Bet she wants to get the man to talk. "We had to practice a lot for the recitations? Did you like them? We learned a lot about our local history."

We wait. The man tucks his hands in his pockets, turns his head and cranes his neck like he's trying to see the horizon. Doesn't want to answer my question. Hmm. Now, what do we do?

With Marian's mouth closed, I jump in. "I've got to take another look at that treasure. That emerald is something you don't see around here very often. Have you seen it?" The tall one's eyes shift from the horizon to Marian.

I turn to go into the church with Marian and Ahmik close behind. Got to see if the gem is still there. Maybe it's already been taken. Another couple and their children pass us on their way out. The two men are part of our group. We all go in. One by one, we take out places in front of the table. I glance at the man with the odd hat – the hat I saw on the figure that was on the cliff when I got buried under the driftwood. His hands rest on his belly. His eyes try to absorb the treasure.

"What a jewel!" I control my voice. "We're going to return it to its owner."

"Peter, maybe we should . . ." I have no idea what Marian is about to say or do. The man puts his hand out then pulls it back quickly. Oh, no. He's going for the gem. I've got to do something fast.

"Would you like to hold the gem?" I ask. The man's head jerks around. Does he understand what I just said? I don't know if it makes sense myself. I try again, "The people in town got to hold the gem, would you like to examine it?"

His yo-yo head moves slowly as he hisses, "Yessssss. I would."

I think Marian and Ahmik are still beside me, but I'm not sure. I can't take my eyes off the man, his over-sized hand, and the emerald. My body is shaking, but I know I've got to do it. I've got to put the gem in his hand. I've got to take a chance.

"Put your hand out and I'll put the gem in the palm of your hand. Please be careful. Don't drop it." I pick up the emerald in slow motion. Its cold surface tries to freeze what I'm about to do. "Are you ready?"

An old weathered hand unfolds before me making a cradle. What a giant hand. My hand holding the jewel with two fingers moves at the speed of maple sap in winter toward its target – his palm. I put the jewel down. I hold my breath. I can see him if I tilt my head up just a bit. He's absolutely still, just looking, looking deeply into the sea of deep green that shines in his hand. His friend moves in to take a look. Does he want to hold it too? I'm definitely not sure what's going to happen next. Maybe they'll try to run out the door. Hope one of the guards is outside. I glance over to the corner, and Martin is standing where Jacob stood before. His eyes are as big as the moon.

"Stories tell of pirates who buried it in the sand after their ship went down." Again nothing. Now what should I say?

I steal a peek at Marian who for once in her life is speechless, and Ahmik is silent, but watching.

A deep raspy voice crawls its way out of the hunched-over man, his hand still out in front of him.

"I know." The words are barely audible. My mind whirls in confusion.

I can't form words from my mixed-up thoughts. One by one, words take shape in the old man's mouth then he speaks, "I know . . . I'm . . . I'm the pirate who stole . . . who took the box." My knees begin to buckle. My moist hands hang at my sides. All I can do is think about our plan for capturing someone who is supposed to steal the treasure. I . . . what do I do now?

The church door creaks open. Someone clears his throat. That's Pa's sound, but I can't turn around.

"I'm . . . sorry for what I did. I was young then. Now I . . ." Trembling hands, trembling words, a trembling spirit stand before me.

"My name's Ben - Benjamin Hornigold. I hope you'll help me return this jewel to Lady Jane."

He's not going to steal the jewel. I can't believe it. There's . . . there's no one to capture.

"Yes, yes, we . . ." My words stick to the roof of my mouth. I don't know what to say next.

"You are very brave and kind, Peter." The would-be thief smiles for the first time. I smile back.

"Of course I will. My friends will too. Everyone in this town will, especially Pa." The old pirate turns to face me. The gem still rests in his hand.

"Are . . . are you fi . . . finished looking at the gem?" My words trip over themselves. He nods. I pick up the emerald and place it carefully in its beautiful signature box. I stare at the gem. It's like looking into a deep pine forest and at the same time at new leaves on an apple tree. So beautiful and now it's safe.

* * *

Ahmik, Marian and I sit on the edge of the bluff.

"Look at those piles of driftwood. They give me shivers when I think of how they fell on me and I almost lost my life here."

"You were very lucky," Ahmik says softly. "Your dog is very special just like you. He brought you help. He saved your life, friend." A smile creeps across my face.

"The beach below is the beach of hidden treasure." Marian's voice comes to our ears just like the sound of the waves.

"Did you know these waves breaking over the rocks sank pirate ships?" My voice quivers just thinking about those ships.

"We have more history to add to our recitations – we have a story about an eagle," Ahmik says proudly. My lips smile along with my heart.

"Look at what has happened. An old pirate confessed his crime and wants to return the jewel."

"And what's in the future, Peter," Marian asks.

"Lady Jane will recover her father's gift, and the townspeople will let Ben and Stanley become part of our town."

"And you, Peter?" Ahmik peers into my eyes as if looking into the future.

"Me? Well, I . . . I'm going to spend time with my trusted friends. We have a lot more to explore . . . in the past." Marian's smile reaches out to the horizon and Ahmik, with his eyes closed, begins to chant softly.